Love is
a time of enchantment:
in it all days are fair and all fields
green. Youth is blest by it,
old age made benign:
the eyes of love see
roses blooming in December,
and sunshine through rain. Verily
is the time of true-love
a time of enchantment — and
Oh! how eager is woman
to be bewitched!

FAIR ROSALIND

When Rosalind Fenner-Smith travels to Norfolk with her mother, she encounters the local landowner and tyrant, Sheldon Howard, Marquis of Langton, who lives with his frivolous sister, Letitia, on their large estate. The Marquis's plans to flood the village to create a lake in his grounds is causing uproar amongst the villagers. The young rector, Simon Throckmorton, is violently opposed to the scheme, but he has the misfortune to win the love of the wayward Lady Letitia. Her brother disapproves and chaos ensues. Rosalind sets about putting matters right, but soon finds events running out of control.

Books by V. M. D. Rowlands
Published by The House of Ulverscroft:

THE LADY AND THE HIGHWAYMAN

V. M. D. ROWLANDS

FAIR ROSALIND

354892

Complete and Unabridged

ULVERSCROFT
Leicester

First published in Great Britain in 1984 by
Robert Hale Limited
London

First Large Print Edition
published 1997
by arrangement with
Robert Hale Limited
London

British Library CIP Data

Rowlands, V. M. D.
    Fair Rosalind.—Large print ed.—
Ulverscroft large print series: romance
1. Love stories
2. Large type books
I. Title
823.9'14 [F]

ISBN 0–7089–3869–8

Published by
F. A. Thorpe (Publishing) Ltd.
Anstey, Leicestershire

Set by Words & Graphics Ltd.
Anstey, Leicestershire
Printed and bound in Great Britain by
T. J. International Ltd., Padstow, Cornwall

This book is printed on acid-free paper

1

ON St Valentine's Day, 14th February, in the year 1797, towards sunset, on a ship of His Britannic Majesty's Navy engaged in the Battle of Cape St Vincent, a certain gallant Captain Jocelyn Fenner-Smith died of wounds received during the action, thus ending a distinguished career of service to his country. He was buried at sea with all due ceremony, and his few personal belongings were sent back to England to his wife and daughter.

★ ★ ★

In a tall house in London, in a respectable but unfashionable part of the town, lived Mrs Jocelyn Fenner-Smith and her only daughter. Mrs Fenner-Smith was a plain, sensible, unremarkable woman, fifty years of age, the daughter of a strict Methodist middle-class banker from Birmingham. Her figure was matronly, her stature rather short, her face kindly, her dark hair turning to grey. Her daughter was twenty-seven, called Rosalind, an incongruous name for such a young woman, for she had a face like a horse, the figure of an Amazon, and long, crinkly pale red hair. She had pale blue eyes, a prominent nose, rather protruding teeth, and wore unbecoming spectacles. Her redeeming features were a flawless, perfect creamy skin, and a heart of gold, though it beat beneath a very downright, organizing manner. She spent her time setting the world to rights, doing good works, and distributing charity to the poor and needy. Such was her benevolence and goodwill that amongst those who had benefited from it she was nick-named 'Fair Rosalind!'.

Mother and daughter lived very quietly and modestly and happily, the only blight to that happiness being the absence of a beloved husband and father away at sea serving his country most of the time. Therefore, news of his death in the Battle of Cape St Vincent, though such a thing was always an accepted possibility, nevertheless came as a severe blow to them. But being the strong-minded women they were, they sobbed out their grief, then packed their belongings, closed up the London house, and dutifully set out to visit the late Captain's father, Sir Philip Fenner-Smith, at Harford Grange in Hertfordshire.

"How do you suppose Grandpapa will have taken the news?" Rosalind remarked, as the chaise bore them up the long winding drive to the Grange.

"You know your grandfather, dear," Mrs Fenner-Smith returned. "He is a hard-hearted old man, else he had not turned off your poor Uncle Michael the way he did, and not had sight nor sound of him since. No, there was no love lost between Grandpapa and his sons, yet I am persuaded he will be sorry for Papa's death. Of course, it will make it prodigious awkward for him, your uncle now being his sole heir."

"I see how it is," Rosalind said feelingly. "Poor Uncle Michael. Think you he has been acquainted with Papa's death?"

"I doubt it, my love. I have no notion where he is. I do not know if

3

even Grandpapa has knowledge of his whereabouts. Of course, he will have to be told."

"Do you remember him, Mama? I must confess I cannot recollect him."

"That is scarce surprising, since you were only twelve years old when you last saw him. We never had much to do with him; he always kept himself to himself. And after he ran off with that dreadful woman — "

"Oh dear! I fear Papa's death could not have been more inopportune. It will rake up so many old memories and bitternesses."

"It is up to us, Rosalind, you and I, to smooth over the breach between your uncle and your grandpapa. It may not be easy, Uncle Michael having become something of a recluse since his wife left him, but it is clearly our duty."

"Yes, Mama. As soon as we have waited upon Grandpapa, we will find my uncle and break the news to him."

Thus it was that a week later mother and daughter found themselves in Sir Philip Fenner-Smith's rather ancient carriage bound for Norfolk. The old

4

gentleman had indeed been greatly cut up over the death of his eldest son, had acknowledged the need to establish some kind of relationship with his other son, but had refused point-blank to have any communication with him himself, at least at this point.

"How I wish you had been a boy, Rosalind," the old man said, misty-eyed. She was the apple of his eye, had made up to him for all the disappointment of his sons, and could do no wrong as far as he was concerned. "I would have gladly had you as my heir, but as things are, my title and estates must all go to — to my other son." He could not even bring himself to mention Michael by name. "I could only wish to see you well set up in life, married to some rich gentleman — "

"I am quite happy as I am, dear Grandpapa," she assured him, squeezing his hand. "Besides, no one could possibly wish to marry a — a *horse*." She laughed loudly at herself. "I really am the ugliest female alive, you know."

"Beauty is in the eye of the beholder, my child," Sir Philip remarked. "I am old enough to have learnt that much. And to me you are exceeding beautiful, Rosalind. Your skin is like peaches and cream." He lightly fingered her cheek. "And your hair is like rippled sand after the receding tide has washed it."

"Oh, stuff!" the prosaic Miss Fenner-Smith exclaimed. "How you do go on, Grandpapa." Nevertheless, she was greatly touched by such genuine compliments, and only wished her grandfather might think so highly of poor Uncle Michael. She changed the subject abruptly. "Now pray do try and recall, sir. Do you know where my uncle resides now? He must be acquainted with Papa's death directly."

"It is the oddest thing, do you know, dear child," he said ruminatively, rising to his feet and hobbling over to his desk, which he began rummaging through, "but I had a letter from him only the other day, the first in near a dozen years. After all this time he begs my forgiveness for what he did, for running off with another man's wife — "

"They weren't actually *married*, Grandpapa," Rosalind felt moved to make the point clear.

"As near as dammit, miss. The girl threw over her affianced husband for my son. It amounts to the same thing."

"Not quite, sir. My uncle did marry her — "

"And she subsequently left him. Tut, girl, it is a miserable tale. I want no part of it. My sympathies are all with the poor young fellow she so heartlessly jilted. But I dare say my son has since reaped his own reward. I will receive him — in time. You may tell him that from me."

"I shall be most happy to do so, sir, but where *is* he?"

"Gone to ground in East Anglia, my dear, it seems. Let me see — Ah, yes, here, I have it." He fished out a letter and held it up triumphantly, then peered at it short-sightedly. "Norfolk, yes, that is it, Norfolk, of all outlandish places. Somewhere called — er — um — New Lyng, near Fakenham. I must confess to having never heard of it. He calls his house Long Croft, whatever kind of a house that may be. You will go there for me, Rosalind, and give him my blessing?"

"Oh, *yes*, Grandpapa, of a surety," she cried happily.

"But I will not see him yet awhile, you understand? In my own time — "

"Yes, Grandpapa."

"Then you had best make haste and go tomorrow. He should not be kept in ignorance of events any longer."

★ ★ ★

In remote Norfolk, at Lyng House, the seat of the Marquis of Langton, situated between Kings Lynn and Fakenham, news of the Battle of Cape St Vincent did not arrive until Saturday, 4th March, and then caused very little comment, Lord Langton being much preoccupied with his own problems.

"Conceive of it, Sheldon," his sister Letitia, who had brought the news to him, said enthusiastically, "a victory at last. I dare say this horrid war will not last so very much longer now."

"What's that?" Lord Langton returned blankly, looking up at last from the papers he was studying.

"Why, I do not believe you have heard a word I said," Letitia said crossly.

"I do not think I have." My lord

was not at all apologetic, merely very downright. "Must you keep interrupting me?"

"I beg your pardon, but you really should take more interest in the affairs of the nation and less in your own. That is what you are for ever telling me."

Sheldon snapped down the pencil he was holding and looked up sharply.

"Say what you have to say, Letty, and then pray have the goodness to be quiet," he said shortly. Immediately his dark eyes dropped back to the papers before him, and he ended viciously: "I'm damned if I'll permit him to have his confounded Sunday School in any property of mine while he continues to refuse to cooperate with me about diverting the river across his meadow."

"It *is* his meadow, at least while he is the incumbent of the Rectory, and if you divert the river it will very likely cause excessively bad flooding, much more than usual, every time it rains, besides which you would very probably dry up his water supply, and that of half the village as well, and you do only want to make an ornamental lake which will give pleasure to no one but yourself. You are prodigious selfish, Sheldon."

"It is none of your business, in any event," Lord Langton said abruptly. "You listen too much to village gossip. What were you saying about Cape St Vincent?"

"Oh, so you did hear in part what I said?" Letitia retorted, a trifle contemptuously, but wisely, from long experience of her difficult brother's bad temper, abandoning the subject of the Rector and his meadow. "I said that we have just heard great news. Admiral Sir John Jervis was engaged in battle with the Spanish Fleet, and won a glorious victory over them. The Spaniards were defeated completely, and four of their ships were taken. Is that not good news indeed, brother?"

"Assuredly so, but not before time, and it is hardly a subject you should be bothering yourself with. You would be better employed about your womanly duties, such as making sure that my dinner is not near cold when it arrives at table as it was yesterday."

"Oh, you are pig-headed and impossible,

Sheldon," Letitia stormed, "and if I had your dinner here right now I should fling it at your head."

She ran from the library, where he was sitting, and slammed the door after her. The vibration caused a small porcelain figurine to wobble precariously on its high shelf, and then crash to the floor and smash to smithereens.

"*Damn* the female!" Lord Langton exclaimed angrily, getting up to tug furiously at the bell pull to order a servant to sweep up the mess immediately. His summons was answered at once, for his staff knew better than to keep him waiting for fear of instant dismissal if he was in a bad mood, which he invariably was, particularly of late since the Rev. Mr Throckmorton had dared to oppose his will.

The interruption over, Lord Langton resumed his seat at his desk and began studying the map of the parish again, absent-mindedly chewing the end of his pencil and frowning at the papers. At 33, he was tall and dark and well-built, with a rather frowning, discontented countenance, hard brown eyes and a strong but self-willed mouth. His features were regular and comely, if only he were disposed to smile more. He was very rich, very cultured, very selfish, and very determined, a hard taskmaster and not much liked by his staff, tenants, or neighbours. Following his pursuit of pleasure rather than improvement, his latest whim was to change the course of the little river Lyng that crossed his estate, to divert it into an existing small pond to make an ornamental lake to improve the view from his drawing-room windows. He cared little for the fears of the villagers that by so doing he would greatly increase the chances of disastrous flooding in an area prone to flooding, or that he would disrupt the village water supply.

It was not the first time his family had been at odds with the local inhabitants. Seventy years or more ago, in his great-grandfather's day, when Lyng House was in the course of construction, the old village had stood too close to the noble pile, spoiling the whole effect of such a handsome Palladian building, so the then Lord Langton had solved the problem by simply wiping the whole settlement from the face of the earth and rebuilding it in its proper place, at a discreet distance from the house, beyond the park gates. New Lyng village was now a uniform street of prim orderly pairs of white cottages, ending in the massive white iron gates of Lyng House. At least in the 1720s the villagers had gained new dwellings out of the noble lord's whim, this time they would gain nothing and very likely stand to lose much. And all that stood between them and Lord Langton's so called tyranny and possible disaster was their new Rector, the Rev. Mr Simon Throckmorton, and his little meadow.

Lord Langton swore violently, and angrily snapped his pencil in half. No way could he see to divert the river conveniently to suit his purpose without crossing the Rector's meadow. And the worst of it was, the living was not even his to bestow, so he could not even turn the confounded fellow out and put someone more amenable in his place. And now the young puppy had had the impudence to come to him begging leave to start a Sunday School in the small building that had once been a charity school and now stood empty and half derelict, a building that belonged to the Lyng House estate. Well, he'd see how badly the young upstart wanted his precious Sunday School, coming to the erstwhile peaceful village and stirring up discontent and unrest with his fancy notions. The Rev. Mr Throckmorton had a thing or two to learn about his new neighbour the Marquis of Langton.

There was a timid knock at the door. Lord Langton started up and swore violently again, but his expression changed slightly as the servant announced tonelessly: "Mrs Montagu, my lord."

A rather hard-faced, very self-possessed young woman trod purposefully into the room.

"Oh, it's you, Josephine," Sheldon said, not very graciously, but at least in a tone of voice that accepted her presence. "What the devil do you want?"

Josephine Montagu was the wife of a neighbouring squire (a man much older than herself), the mother of five children, and Lord Langton's mistress (the last of her offspring being reputed to be his). She was very fashionable in a high-waisted redingote that showed off her trim figure to advantage, and a dashing plumed turban sat on her gleaming russet curls. Her eyes were blue and hard, her nose aquiline and haughty, her mouth tight and rather thin-lipped, but for all that she was generally considered a beautiful woman.

"Aren't you pleased to see me, Sheldon?" she asked, putting hcr cheek up to him to be kissed.

"I am in no mood for chit-chat," he replied shortly, dutifully pecking her on the cheek.

"Are you ever?" she responded with a slight smile, as she stripped off her gloves. "But you ought to know me better by now than to suppose I indulge in idle chatter. No, I have come to offer you my advice."

He raised a dark brow at her in surprise.

"Oh! What about, pray? Because I dare say I can well do without it."

"You really are the most obnoxious man, Sheldon. Why I bother with you I don't know."

"Because I can give you what your husband cannot," he said bluntly. "Well, what of this advice of yours?"

A bright spot of angry colour had appeared in her rouged cheeks, but she only said with marvellous calm: "Have you forgot Long Croft?"

"What?" he ejaculated. "Long Croft? What has that to say to anything?"

"You have the most annoying habit of repeating things, Sheldon. It really does not become you. I shall think you are growing senile."

"Saucy baggage!" he cried, with a sudden shout of amused laughter. "Senile, indeed! I'll soon show you just how senile I am when next I get you in bed. But what's this about Long Croft? You mean that absurd Gothic cottage that stands alone at the end of the village street, where Crazy Mick lives?"

"Crazy Mick, as you so derisively call him, happens to be the son of a baronet," Josephine informed him tartly.

"Does he, by God! I never knew that. Who'd have believed it? For all that, he's still as mad as a hatter. Why all this sudden interest in Long Croft and Crazy

16

Mick? The place is a modern monstrosity in the worst of bad taste, and if it had been on my land I should never have suffered it to be built at all."

"But it is *not* on your land, and that is the very point I wish to make. Have you never studied the map properly, Sheldon? For a man of your intelligence, I am surprised at you. Here you have been all this time falling out with the Rector about his precious meadow, when all you have to do is divert the river the other way, across Long Croft land. See, here," she added, pointing out the spot on the map laid out on his desk.

"Good lord, d'you suppose I had not thought of that?" he remarked, nevertheless studying the map more closely again. "That way it would be miles round, and cost a fortune to do. Though I must admit I had not given much serious thought to that proposition. It is so far round I had not conceived it a viable proposition, let alone considered whose land it was all round there. I had no idea so much land even belonged to Long Croft. How do you know?"

"Because my husband was the one who

sold it to Crazy Mick when he built Long Croft."

"Well, I'll be dashed!"

"And I am persuaded Crazy Mick would be easier game than the Rev. Mr Throckmorton. You cannot *really* wish to carry on a feud with the Rector, Sheldon, can you, or make yourself so unpopular with the villagers?"

"That is of little import to me," he replied carelessly. "Besides, they all exaggerate the issue. There has always been flooding in New Lyng. What it all boils down to is the fact that our worthy Rector does not want to accommodate me in any way. I dare say he is a sharp thinking radical, and wishes merely to frustrate me at all turns because I am a landowner."

"He is of very lowly stock, certainly," Mrs Montagu agreed. "His father was a mere curate, and his grandfather a common clerk."

"How do you know?" Sheldon demanded, rather taken aback.

"I make it my business to find out such things, my dear." She smiled in a self-satisfied way. "The trouble with you is you have no subtlety. You charge about like a mad bull, instead of taking time to get all the facts first."

"You are full of criticism of me today, Josephine," Lord Langton remarked, straightening up to look at her full in the face. "You have called me obnoxious and senile, accused me of repeating things, of not using my intelligence, and of having no subtlety. I must be losing my touch, is that it?"

"How absurd you are, Sheldon. Of course it is no such thing."

"So I am absurd as well now, am I?" he shot at her.

"Pray do not snap me up so," she began, and then broke off laughing. "Wretch! You are roasting me." She hit his arm reprovingly with her gloves. "Really, it will not do. Next you will have the Rev. Mr Throckmorton accuse you of frivolity."

"He has accused me of everything else in the book," Sheldon remarked with a smile that lit up his habitual dour expression and made him look quite pleasant. "He has now quite given up all pretence at politeness and neighbourliness with me. I do believe we have arrived at a point of open hostility which is most regrettable."

"Unless you heed my advice. Do you know, Sheldon," she added in surprise, "I really do believe you do not like falling out with Mr Throckmorton. I had not thought you cared a jot."

"Dammit, woman, of course I care!" Lord Langton cried violently. "Do you think I *like* being constantly at daggers drawn with everybody? It's too deuced uncomfortable by far."

"Then if that is the case, my dear, why do you always set people's backs up so?"

"Rather, I think, is the boot on the other foot," he retorted uncompromisingly. "It is others who set *my* back up. I will not tolerate being thwarted at all. Now, what would you have me do? Go wait upon Crazy Mick, is that it?"

"No, not yet. Let me go first. Or perhaps we should go together. Yes, that is it. We must go together. Only let me do the talking, for he is scarce acquainted with you — "

"I wouldn't know him from Adam,"

Sheldon interrupted.

"And you would be bound to say the wrong thing and overset him at the outset," Josephine finished firmly. "He is a trifle slow, poor man, and you know what a hasty temper you have, Sheldon."

"There you go, Josephine, finding fault with me again," he accused, though with that same amused smile. "Small wonder your husband is such a poor creature if you are such a shrew at home."

She wisely ignored this taunt, instead slowly and deliberately taking off her turban, setting it on an occasional table, and herself sitting primly on a hard-backed chair.

"You cannot suppose I mean to go this very minute, Sheldon," she announced firmly. "Are you not going to provide me with some refreshment? I have come out specially for you in all this cold wind."

"I did not ask you to," he returned bluntly. "In any event, you can have felt little of either cold or wind, since you only had to step into your carriage at one end and out of it at the other."

"Ungrateful, unfeeling wretch!" she snapped. "Pray ring for tea to be brought to me at once," she added imperiously.

"I will do no such thing," he flung back angrily. "What do you take me for? Ring for it yourself if you want it. You usually do make free with my house, anyway."

"You are no gentleman, Sheldon," she cried, suddenly as furious as he, her hard bright eyes glinting angrily.

"There, madam, you are far out. I am every bit a gentleman, else I should have had you flung out long since at such ill-bred caterwauling in my library."

They glowered at each other ferociously for a moment, till she turned away, exclaiming in disgust: "*Oh!*"

She sat tapping her foot impatiently, waiting for him to speak again. At times she almost hated him. He was callous, completely selfish, with a heart of stone. He was even a cruel lover, as many of the young serving wenches and village girls he had reputedly ruined had found out to their cost. There was a small scar on his left cheek, a reminder of a duel he had once fought with the husband of his then mistress. She knew she was playing with fire with him. One day even her tolerant, slow-witted husband might turn, and that day not so far off, for he had been cutting up rough of late, and had not lain with her for months. Sheldon Howard fascinated her. He was a man of breeding, of taste and intelligence, and had the courage of his convictions, even if they were not always the right ones. In short, he was everything her poor Mr Montagu was not.

Sheldon, regarding her handsome aquiline profile while he recovered his temper, thought what a mean, grasping woman she was. He was beginning to tire of her imperious ways. She thought she owned him. One of these days she was in for a rude awakening. He would tell her, quite bluntly, that he had had enough of her, and if she did not like it above half, she must do the other thing. That was the trouble, he reflected. Life for him was getting stale. Years ago, before the war, he had spent most of his time jaunting round Italy, Greece, Egypt. The ancient world held a strong fascination for him.

Now the conflict in Europe kept him at home, and he was reduced to a paltry squabble with the local Rector to gain excitement. He didn't really give a damn about diverting the River Lyng, though the resulting change of scene would have given him pleasure, and of course he did not want to upset anyone's water supply or flood their land if possible. Rather the opposite. He was not an inhuman monster, as the Rev. Mr Throckmorton tried to make out. But he did hate to be thwarted, and the young whippersnapper with all his high-flown prosing had put his back up at the outset, which had made him determined to fight it out to the bitter end and not be beaten. And if Josephine Montagu could help him to that end, she still had her uses for him, and must not be upset too much.

"Very well, I will ring for tea for you, Josephine," he returned at length. "And in return you will tell me all you know of Crazy Mick, and of our friend the Rector."

"Thank you, Sheldon," she said graciously.

He rang for tea, and then sat on the

edge of the desk, swinging one leg. He picked up an orange from a silver bowl and began idly peeling it.

"Well?" he said sharply.

She looked surprised. "I did not suppose that you were serious, for I cannot believe that anything I tell you can really be of any significance to you in the case."

"Nevertheless, I wish to know," he returned uncompromisingly. "I doubt Crazy Mick is so crazy as is generally believed, merely because he builds an unusual house and keeps himself to himself. I respect his privacy. He is probably not such easy game as you seem to imagine."

"Why do you defend him all at once," she cried, with a slight return of anger, "when you yourself have just said you wouldn't know him from Adam? It is not like you, Sheldon, to make up to people, even to gain your own ends. You are usually far too busy abusing them. But I will tease you no further, for I perceive you are like to lose your temper again else, and that I cannot countenance. Your Crazy Mick is properly termed

Captain Michael Fenner-Smith, late of His Majesty's Ship *Arbruthnot*."

"A Navy man, eh?" Lord Langton commented with alert interest. "Well, well! The fellow's a dark horse indeed. What else, pray?"

"Not much. He is a bachelor or a widower, for he has no wife. His father is Sir Philip Fenner-Smith of Harford Grange in Hertfordshire, and I believe he has a brother still serving at sea."

"So why did he choose to retire to this remote part of the world if his family hail from Hertfordshire, I wonder?"

"That, Sheldon, you must find out for yourself. I dare say there is nothing to it in the least. He probably likes the scenery, or else he fell out with his father."

"That sounds more reasonable to me," Sheldon said, rather dourly, as he thoughtfully ate his orange. "I hear we have won a great victory off Cape St Vincent," he abruptly changed the subject. "I had no notion until my sister informed me of it. I see I shall have to apply myself more to studying the affairs of the nation instead of merely my own.

I am getting too provincial by far."

"That is one thing you will never be, Sheldon," Josephine said decidedly. "You are by far too clever, far too knowledgeable, and far too worldly-wise. You cannot have rubbed shoulders so much with the ancient world and the world of art as you have and call yourself provincial."

"You flatter me too much, my dear. I have had a few jaunts to Greece and Egypt and the like, and I have a passing acquaintance with the arts, but that hardly makes me a connoisseur, and certainly does not save me from being odiously provincial at times."

"You are too modest," she retorted with spirit. "But then I suppose that is no bad thing. You must be allowed some good attributes, and modesty might well be one of them. You are not much given to blowing your own trumpet."

"But *that*, no doubt, is because I have nothing to blow it about," he added, with a rare smile.

Over tea, they sat companionably discussing the arts, a subject which invariably put Lord Langton in a good mood, and eventually Mrs Montagu made as if to depart, promising to return on Monday to escort his lordship to Long Croft to introduce him to Crazy Mick.

2

IT was a bright, blustery March day, very cold, the north east wind whipping across the countryside as only it can in Norfolk, and Lord Langton was restless. As soon as she had finished her tea, he practically pushed Josephine out of the house, much to her rage, for she had come fully expecting him to accept her favours as he usually did when she visited him. It infuriated her that he should so reject her whenever it suited him. But to preserve her dignity she went at his bidding. She had no wish to cause a scene, or to fall out with him at such a time. She had not yet told him, but she was breeding again, and there could be no doubt that he was responsible this time. She dreaded the day she must tell him, for there had been scenes enough before, and he had thrown her over till her husband had accepted the child as his.

For a while after she had gone, Sheldon sat studying his map, then on sudden impulse he got up and decided to go out, sending imperious orders to the stables to have the large grey mare saddled and ready for him.

Lyng House was a handsome, early Palladian grey stone mansion standing four-square in its park, with the close-mown grass coming right up to the house on all sides. In each corner it was topped by a cupola, and flanked on either side by curving colonnaded wings linking it to two square blocks housing the kitchens, servants' quarters, the orangery, and the like. To the North a broad tree-lined grass avenue stretched away to the fields beyond. From the South Front a split flight of shallow stone steps descended to a gravel path. The stable block lay right away from the house. It was an elegant classical erection of modest red brick, set round a cobbled courtyard in the middle of which was a fountain playing into a deep bath-like basin.

When Lord Langton strode under the high archway into the courtyard, the grey mare had already been saddled and led out to await him. The head groom no less than the lowest stable lad scurried to do his least bidding, and he thought dourly how the thin veneer of civilization was only held in place by the rule of fear. Were it not for the fact that he had the power of dismissal over his menials, no doubt they would never do a thing he told them, or show him the least deference, for he knew they disliked him cordially. And *they* knew that nowhere else would they get such high wages, and that if they were turned off on no account would he give them a reference to get another post. Not for him the old family retainer who worked for love. Had he been in France, he was sure he would have been a guest of Madame la Guillotine long ago.

Not that he didn't have his problems, apart from the matter of Mr Throckmorton and his infernal meadow. Of his large family of younger sisters, all were now safely married, except Letitia. And she was a problem no man deserved, at least in his estimation. For one thing, Letty was still under age, and, their parents both being long dead, he was her legal guardian. He had practically brought her up, in fact. It was a fact that did not seem to have done her any good. She was wild and wilful and quite unmanageable. She enraged him in private and disgraced him in public. Despite his hasty temper, he was usually a perfect gentleman, his address most correct, and to have a wild creature like Letty about him, shocking her audience with her outrageous speech and behaviour, was most mortifying to him. Not only did it show him up, his lack of control over her, it also put him greatly at fault in his upbringing of her. The fact that he was really very fond of her did not help, for only by playing the heavyhanded older brother could he ever discipline her at all, and that was a role he detested, at least with her, for it only made her dislike him and kick over the traces all the more at other times. Why could she not have been conventional, biddable, ladylike, like all his other sisters? If only he could find a suitable husband for her, but so far she had flatly refused to marry anyone, though many had sought her hand, for she was exceedingly well endowed.

In the past he had tried engaging a female companion for her, but that had not worked out. Now he was nearing his wits' end, for he was not a patient man, and she had tried him sorely these past few months. He had sent her to her aunt's in Bath, but she had come home again after only two weeks, declaring she had died of boredom with that whey-faced old harridan. Now she was plaguing the life out of him and he knew she would stop at nothing to torment him, even hurt him if the opportunity arose. And since she had found out about his affair with Mrs Montagu — Well, he was far more vulnerable than he had believed possible. After all these years he had thought he was past such weaknesses. But in truth he found himself as capable of being hurt as he had been years ago when Amelia had so cruelly jilted him.

He winced at the memory. "You are a selfish, heartless, callous *pig*, and love only yourself," her angry words came back to him. Perhaps that had been so, but he had not meant to be. He had loved her with all his heart, and had tried to prove it to her in every way possible, but in the end he had realized she had not cared a jot for him and had only been attracted by his wealth and position. But even that had not been enough for her, and a few days before their wedding she had run off with a half-pay Navy officer. It had come as a severe blow to his youthful pride and an even greater hurt to his heart to discover that the female he adored found him so odious she could not bear to marry him.

That was all a long time ago, though. He had had many women since then, but had never loved one again, and so had supposed he could never be hurt by one again. Only Letty's taunts had caught him on the raw, opening up old wounds, and lately he found himself reliving past moments that evoked nothing but pain. The result was that he was often sharper than he meant to be with Letty, and this did nothing to improve relations between them. It was a vicious circle, all very distressing.

Sheldon rode at a gallop across the park. The wildness of the wind whipping across his face exactly suited his mood. The Rectory stood the other side of the lane that bordered the park. It was a modest red-brick Queen Anne house with rounded arched windows, standing in a neat garden of lawns and shrubs and trees, with the fateful meadow beyond. Lord Langton drew rein before it and surveyed it, as if by so doing he could miraculously change the course of the River Lyng across it.

All at once the front door of the Rectory opened, and a young man with a pale face, large nose, and pale sandy hair, wearing clerical black, came out. He strode across to his white front gate, calling out as he did so:

"Good-day to you, my lord. I had not expected to be honoured by a visit from your lordship today."

"I am not come to visit you, sir," Sheldon snapped at once. "I am merely passing by."

"That is not how it appears to me, my lord," the Rev. Mr Throckmorton said with almost bare-faced insolence.

"I stopped to admire the view," Sheldon retorted crushingly. "You do not object, I trust. But since when was I accountable to you for my actions?"

"You are when it comes to my meadow or the welfare of my parishioners, my lord," Mr Throckmorton returned, with heightened colour.

"You presume too much, sir," Lord Langton said angrily. "Permit me to remind you that I have been here far longer than you. Indeed, my family has been here for five hundred years."

"Then perhaps, my lord, you and yours have been here *too* long," the Rector said boldly.

"Confound you for an impudent upstart, sir. You will do well to look to your own business and leave me to mine."

"Your lordship is one of my flock," young Mr Throckmorton said, rather pompously, though he did not mean it to sound that way, "and your spiritual welfare *is* my business. Your association with Mrs Montagu is highly irregular, a bad example to the villagers, and distresses me beyond everything — "

"Poppycock!" Sheldon interrupted with furious contempt. "That is not the way to get my permission for your confounded Sunday School. Go to the devil, sir!"

He dug his heels sharply into his

horse's flanks and rode away at a great rate.

So the impudent fellow was presuming to lecture him now, was he? he thought angrily. That was something he would not tolerate. He would not have any young whippersnapper of a parson moralizing at him, and certainly not the Rev. Mr Simon Throckmorton. He would have to be put in his place once and for all. He was becoming a thorn in the flesh.

Lord Langton's thoughts were dark and vengeful, his expression likewise, as he rounded the bend in the lane that followed the park railings and passed the magnificent, impressive great white gates of the main entrance to Lyng House. They were flanked on either side by trim white lodges. Opposite these, another road turned off at sharp right angles to climb up a slight incline through the street of the earlier Lord Langton's model village to the tree-lined approach beyond. At the end of the orderly pairs of white cottages, standing apart from the rest of the dwellings on the right hand side of the road, at the end of a long wooded garden, was Long Croft, a large, romantic cottage built in the Gothic revival style, with thatched roof and pointed arched windows like those of a church. It still looked starkly new, despite the darkness of the Norfolk reeds of its thatch, and its white-washed plaster walls. To Sheldon's eyes it appeared an ugly monstrosity in the most execrable taste.

A man was walking down the winding crazy-paving path to the front gate. He was about forty-five, tall and lean, with rather untidy dark hair loose about his collar, a weather-beaten, deeply-lined face with alert, brilliant blue eyes, a long sharp nose, and a thin-lipped, slightly twisted mouth, as if he was in constant pain. He walked with a decided limp. On seeing Lord Langton, a slow friendly smile spread over his features.

"Good-day, sir. You are looking prodigious out of countenance, if you will forgive my saying so. Are you sorely vexed, pray?"

Lord Langton was completely taken by surprise. He had drawn rein before Long Croft. Now he slid agilely to the ground, and slipped the reins over the gatepost.

His anger had vanished at once. Could this stranger be Crazy Mick? He vaguely seemed to remember hearing that the fellow had a limp. Some old war wound. But this man did not strike him as at all crazy.

"I am sore vexed indeed, sir," he replied at length.

"If there is any way I can help you, sir — " the other began in the same friendly fashion.

"Thank you, but no," Sheldon said quickly. "A mere personal annoyance. But I believe I have not the honour of your acquaintance."

"Captain Fenner-Smith, sir, at your service," Crazy Mick informed him, with an awkward bow.

"Ah, yes. I am pleased to meet you, sir."

"And you, sir?"

"I am Langton of Lyng House. Your servant, sir." He nodded briefly, but his tone was not unpleasant.

"Of course. How remiss of me. I should have known. Pray forgive me, my lord. I have long meant to wait upon you, but I do not go abroad, and in bad weather I am much plagued by this confounded wound in my leg."

"Of course. I understand," Sheldon said, in a surprisingly conciliatory tone for him. "Pray do not regard it, sir. It is I who am grossly at fault. I should have waited upon you long since, but being ignorant of your circumstances — "

Captain Fenner-Smith smiled his twisted smile.

"I am not unaware of what people hereabouts say about me, my lord," he said quietly. "They think I am a little odd, to say the least, because I built this extraordinary cottage and do not stir beyond my own front gate. Unfortunately, my indifferent health will not allow of me to lead a normal life. But it is surprising how ignorance breeds fear. Because the true facts about me are not known, all sorts of peculiarities are attributed to me."

"Very true. I too suffer in part from the same kind of thing. My motives are often misunderstood by the local inhabitants, with the consequence that I am generally held to be a heartless brute. I must confess it often gives me the greatest satisfaction to live up to my reputation." Even now, he reflected, he was in part trying to turn this fellow up sweet with a view to gaining his own ends eventually. For the other part, though, he had to admit in all honesty that he found the Captain strangely likeable for his own sake.

"I do not heed gossip," Crazy Mick was saying. "I take a man as I find him. I would be honoured, my lord, if you would step inside and drink a glass with me, if it is not inconvenient to you."

Inconvenient to him? Sheldon almost laughed out loud. Why, fate was almost playing into his hands. He said, as gravely and politely as he knew how:

"That would be most pleasurable to me, sir."

"I am honoured. If you would care to step this way, my lord."

Sheldon followed Captain Fenner-Smith up the path and in through the pointed arched doorway to the cottage. Inside it was surprisingly light and airy, comfortably furnished with an odd assortment of items, from old sea-chests to elegant pieces of furniture that

41

looked as if they might once have graced a lady's boudoir. Globes and books, charts and a sextant were all jumbled happily together in one corner of the parlour. Lord Langton's quick dark gaze took it all in at a glance. His interest was roused immediately.

"They would think me even odder if they could see this lot," the Captain remarked drily. "All I need is a parrot."

"It is no one's business what a man has, is, or does in the privacy of his own home," Sheldon returned calmly.

"Precisely my own sentiments, my lord." The Captain set a decanter of brandy and two glasses on a small table and poured out two generous measures, handing one to Sheldon.

"His Majesty the King, God bless him!" Captain Fenner-Smith raised his glass in a loyal toast.

Sheldon raised his glass and echoed the sentiment, though personally he thought Farmer George a silly old buffoon, not fit to run his family let alone the country, especially at a time of such crisis as Britain was passing through at present, what with the war abroad, and rising prices and discontent at home. The King should have been put in Bedlam long ago. Still, it was a toast to be expected of a Navy man, and he had no wish to upset the fellow over such an unimportant issue.

"I was in the Royal Navy, you know," the Captain said musingly as he sipped his brandy. "Got this leg in active service years ago when we lost the American colonies back in the eighties."

"I'm sorry," Sheldon said, surprised to find that he really was so. He rarely cared a jot for anyone else, usually being too concerned with himself and his own affairs.

"My brother is still at sea. A fine fellow. Got a wife and grown-up daughter. Though I've not seen any of my family these twelve years and more." A shadow crossed his face. "My father is getting an old man now. I suppose I ought to go and see him, try and patch up old quarrels, but that's not always so easy, is it? Have you any family, sir?"

"One sister at home, several married. Numerous nephews and nieces," the Marquis replied off-handedly. He was not too keen to discuss his own affairs, least of all Letty. The mention of twelve years ago reminded him only too painfully of what he had suffered at the hands of Amelia.

"Ah, yes." The Captain refilled their glasses even more generously than before. Sheldon was glad he had a strong head and reputation for being able to drink most men under the table. He would hate to be obliged either to refuse Crazy Mick's hospitality or else to make a cake of himself.

"I had a wife once," the Captain went on, falling into a mellow, reminiscent mood. "Does that surprise you, my lord?"

"Not at all. Why should it, indeed?"

"I thought, a rum old codger like me, you know." His voice was a little shaky. "In any event, that's what she thought. She left me after only six months. She near broke my heart."

Sheldon was oddly moved. He felt strangely akin to this man, despite the difference in their backgrounds and circumstances. He finished his brandy at a gulp.

"If it's any comfort, sir," he said, rising to go, "I too was once *nearly* married. She ran off and left me at the last moment. She near broke *my* heart."

The Captain's head, that had been drooping slightly, jerked up suddenly, and he looked long and hard at his visitor. For a moment he seemed about to say something, then instead he abruptly raised his glass and exclaimed with much feeling:

"To the devil with all women, sir!"

"Yes, indeed!" Lord Langton said, in complete agreement.

★ ★ ★

The Rev. Mr Simon Throckmorton, going back into his Rectory after his encounter with Lord Langton, was as near to swearing as he considered it proper for a man of God to be. He had not meant to put my lord's back up so, but he had a rather unfortunate forthrightness, besides it did not take much to put the Marquis's back up. The man had a vile, hasty temper, an overbearing, insulting, ill-natured manner, and an unrelenting disposition. For all that, he was one of the flock, if a lost sheep indeed, and it was the duty of God's servant to love, tolerate, and help such a one all he could. The trouble was, my lord did not want to be helped and made it quite impossible for anyone to try.

Mr Throckmorton sighed, and not for the first time wished he was older, wiser and more experienced. Such a one would no doubt be able to handle a man like Langton, and the present situation in particular. And he had other problems, too. Life as an unattached young Rector was not easy. There were all the elderly ladies who wanted to mother him, all the single young ladies who set their caps at him, not to mention the difficulties of running his household affairs, despite the services of an obliging housekeeper. What he needed was a wife, some nice, well-brought-up young woman who would order his life for him and look after his domestic comforts, and be a friend and helpmate to him, as his mother was to his father. But where in his present situation did he find such a woman? And the problem of Lord Langton and his determination to alter the course of the river to feed his proposed ornamental lake was getting more acute. He would not put it past his lordship to go over his head to higher Church authorities over the matter of the Rectory meadow. He really did not know what to do for the best and yet at all costs he must protect the rights and well-being of the villagers against the Marquis's selfish tyranny.

Bother Lord Langton, he thought, as he sat down in his homely parlour to ponder the matter. Outside the tall sash windows the wind was tossing the trees and plants about in the garden immensely. He feared greatly for some of his young shrubs he had recently put in. He had yet to get used to these strong winds they had in this cold, draughty county. He had grown up in Exeter, where there was a vastly different climate.

There were bits of broken twigs scattered about his neat mown lawn, he noticed, and the daffodils were flattened almost to the ground. Such a pity, so heart-breaking to a keen if not very knowledgeable gardener like himself.

All at once he was embarrassed by the sight of his rather elderly housekeeper waddling down the little path to the Necessary House. Oh dear, he really must do something about planting a screen round the place. At least it would make it more discreet. At present it was very obvious. The problem was knowing what best to plant.

Diverted from his other problems, he considered the matter of the Necessary House, and suddenly hit on the notion of going to ask the advice of Captain Fenner-Smith, who was an expert on gardens. He had a great deal of admiration, liking, and respect for the Captain, besides he felt some kinship with him, their both being newcomers and strangers to the district. The man was the kind of person he felt he would like as a friend, if only he were a trifle more forthcoming.

Having made up his mind to wait upon the Captain, Mr Throckmorton duly set out, stopping on his way to visit one or two others of his flock, with the consequence that quite some time had gone by before he arrived at the front gate of Long Croft. Dusk was falling, and a solitary pale light glowed in the parlour window. Tethering his horse to the gatepost where earlier Lord Langton had done exactly the same thing, he trod rather apprehensively up the twisting path. He was not quite sure what his welcome would be, for Crazy Mick was noted for his eccentricities, one of which was that he rarely stirred out-of-doors and did not encourage visitors. But on the few times he, Simon, had called in the way of his pastoral duty, he had been civilly and well received. Now it was slightly different, he had no such excuse.

The Captain himself opened the door, for he lived quite alone, a woman from the village calling in to 'do' for him every day. His lean, deeply-lined face was drawn with pain seemingly not of a purely physical kind, and it appeared and smelt as if he had been drinking.

"Oh!" Mr Throckmorton exclaimed, greatly taken aback and deeply shocked. He hastily recollected himself, adding in as normal a tone as possible: "Good-evening, sir. I am sorry to disturb you at such an hour, but — "

"No matter. Pray do not apologize, sir," the Captain cut him short. "I was about to have some tea. Will you not join me?"

"Thank you, I should be most honoured, sir." Mr Throckmorton stifled a sigh of relief.

Captain Fenner-Smith limped into his cluttered parlour, where a rather stale looking cake, a large tea-kettle, and a cup and plate were set out on a small table. There was also a brandy decanter and two empty glasses, Mr Throckmorton was quick to notice, with a further shock. The older man must have seen his look, for he smiled faintly, and said apologetically:

"I beg you will forgive my untidiness, sir. I am not accustomed to visitors, and you are my second today."

"I am sorry to incommode you — " the Rector began.

"Not at all. The honour and pleasure is all mine, believe me. Lord Langton called upon me, and has not been gone above an hour or so."

"Lord Langton! Good heaven!" Mr

Thockmorton was astounded.

"You sound surprised, sir. I must confess I was all amazement myself."

"Good gracious!" was all the Rector could get out.

"Though to own the truth, it was I invited him in, else he had not stayed, I doubt. I encountered him at my gate."

"Why on earth should such a one bother himself with you, sir, begging your pardon?" Mr Throckmorton asked in his forthright way. "I mean," he added hastily, colouring up at once as he realized what he was saying, "it is not as if you are well acquainted, or he given much to making social calls upon his neighbours. He is a devious fellow and I do not wholly trust his motives. It is greatly to my shame that I must own I cannot like him at all."

"He is a man who suffers much from an unfortunate manner and disposition and an even more unfortunate tendency to be misunderstood. I believe he sustained a great hurt in his early youth. I like him well enough. He is a man of sense."

Mr Throckmorton quite forgot the real purpose of his visit: to ask the

51

Captain's advice about the best kind of trees to plant as a screen round the Rectory Necessary House. Instead he found himself completely diverted by this revelation about Lord Langton.

"Indeed, sir?" he cried now, between disbelief and astonishment. "Forgive me, but I must beg to differ. Have you not heard how he plans to divert the River Lyng to feed his ornamental lake, at great risk to the village water supply, and with the possibility of causing serious flooding hereabouts? I cannot possibly allow such a selfish action, that is why I am refusing him permission to cut across my meadow behind the Rectory. But he has much wealth and power and an utter disregard for others, and is determined to have his own way. Ten to one he will go to higher authority than mine before long. I am vastly worried by it all, and confess myself rather at a stand about it. His lordship will not listen to reason."

"Have you tried getting him to do so, sir?" the Captain put in bluntly. "I am persuaded he would listen very well."

Mr Throckmorton was rather taken aback. No, that was one approach to the problem he had not tried. He had never even supposed that the Marquis would listen to reason, especially from him. Such a possibility was inconceivable, particularly after the pass things had come to between my lord and himself. And yet — Was this the answer to his problem? Captain Fenner-Smith sounded so sure. And he placed great reliance on the Captain's judgment. Could he have been so mistaken in Lord Langton?

"I think, young sir," the older man said gently, "you have fallen prey to village tittle-tattle and grossly misjudged Langton. He only complained to me not long since that he suffers much from having his motives misjudged by the local inhabitants, with the result that he is generally held to be quite heartless. Go wait upon him, in your best and most respectful Sunday manner, and put your case to him. Say I sent you, if you wish, and see if he does not respond."

"He would turn me from his door before I even got there — "

"Nonsense! He is not near so ill-bred."

Mr Throckmorton disagreed, but did

not say so. But to tackle the lion in his den — Why, that would be rashness indeed. And yet —

"I perceive you hesitate, my friend," the Captain commented. "You are unconvinced. Very well. Go home and sleep on it, and come to your decision when your mind is fresh. But mark my words. You will find his lordship quite human and far from heartless. Only pray try and respect his notions."

"Yes, sir," the Rector murmured meekly, feeling very much as if he were a small boy back in school again. And suddenly remembered the real reason why he had come.

Over tea and stale plum cake they discussed the merits of Scotch Fir and English Maple for screening the Necessary House, until Mr Throckmorton recollected he must be about his business. Tomorrow was Sunday and he had to be up early.

That night he pondered on Captain Fenner-Smith's advice, and decided anything was worth a try, even if he himself suffered a severe set-down at his lordship's hands. Duly, therefore, early the next morning before church, on the principle of striking while the iron is hot, he put on his best hat and suit, and set out for Lyng House.

The wind had lessened a bit, but it was still a sprightly March day, with intermittent sunshine breaking through the clouds that were whipping across the wide sky. Mr Throckmorton rode up the long back drive to the mansion, stopping half-way to admire it where it sat four-square to the elements. As he neared the separate stable-block, he debated within himself which door to enter by. Remembering the Captain's advice about having respect for the Marquis, he finally settled on an unobtrusive side door arrived at by going through a small courtyard that housed the pumphouse for the water supply. Observing this, he had a fleeting thought of how vulnerable was his lordship's water supply. One had only to blow up the pumphouse — He pulled himself up short, appalled at his own ideas. This was civilized England, not Revolutionary France in the worst days of the Terror. Were they not at war to prevent such atrocities happening here?

He wasn't quite sure how it happened,

but from the unobtrusive entrance he soon found himself mounting the Great Staircase, a magnificent mahogany structure that climbed three right angles round a bronze statue of a Greek gladiator set on a giant plinth to the balcony above. From a tremendous height hung a massive gilt lantern. Eventually he arrived in the Stone Hall, a massive cube of a room two storeys high with a domed ceiling in classical relief. It got its name from the stone carved walls, the stone balustrade round the balcony that ran all round it, and the beautiful stone frieze work. An immense gilt chandelier was suspended from the high dome. The furniture was gilt and walnut and green velvet by William Kent. Here, amongst so much stately splendour, he rather nervously awaited the Marquis of Langton.

It was with considerable dismay that he was eventually informed that his lordship was not at home, but that his sister, Lady Letitia Howard, would receive him. He would have gone without troubling her ladyship, knowing he had no business with her, but already she was tripping into the room, a vision of saucy loveliness in a daffodil yellow gown caught up under the bosom by a wide green sash with trailing ribbons behind. It set off her dark bobbing curls and bright sparkling brown eyes to great advantage and showed off the unladylike light bronze of her unblemished skin. Something of the devil in her merry smile as she came forward to greet Mr Throckmorton made him feel decidedly uneasy. Heavens, what in the world had he got himself into? Even so, he could not help noticing how enchanting she was, like a wood nymph, or, more correctly, a mischievous sprite. He had seen her before, of course, but never at such close quarters, and never had he been alone with her. Could she and the ill-tempered Lord Langton really have been sired by the same parents? It seemed impossible. And yet there was a definite likeness in the comely, regular features —

"Good-morning, Mr Throckmorton," she said gaily, holding out her hand to him in a most shocking, forward manner. "I am afraid my brother is from home at present. He always rises early. He has gone to wait upon Mrs Montagu," she added outrageously, purposely for the Rector's benefit. "Is he not the most shocking fellow?"

Simon was completely taken aback. This was not at all what he had expected. This was the first time he had done more than pass the time of day with Lady Letitia. He had heard she was a sad romp, a madcap, but even so — Well, he simply had no experience of young ladies who were so brazen and uninhibited. A delicately nurtured young lady should know nothing of her brother's mistresses, and if she did the last thing she should do was talk openly about them.

"Have you quite lost your tongue, sir?" her ladyship teased. "Come now, I promise I won't eat you. What did you want with Sheldon? Was it about your meadow? He is excessively displeased with you, you know, and has sworn vengeance. For a start, he means to stop you starting your Sunday School."

Mr Throckmorton found his voice at last.

"I sincerely trust not, my lady, for I mean to go ahead with it whatever he may say or do." It was not at all what he had come to say, or the attitude he had meant to take, but without even clapping eyes on the Marquis he knew now that his visit was a waste of time. A man of Langton's caste would never listen to reason, or a point of view other than his own.

"You will soon learn, Mr Throckmorton," Lady Letitia said carelessly, "that it does not pay to cross my brother or thwart him in any way."

"Then it is high time that he *was* crossed, ma'am," Mr Throckmorton retorted with some heat and his usual forthrightness, and blushing fierily.

To his amazement the young lady clapped her hands in delight.

"Bravo, sir," she cried. "I am mightily glad to hear you say so. Sheldon is too high-handed by far, and it is time he was taken down a peg and shown the error of his ways. He can be positively odious at times. Pray do not give in to him. Only you will not have to mind what he says or does to you."

"Rest assured, dear lady," Simon said fervently, suddenly filled with a desire to

59

please this engaging miss, "that I shall not budge an inch."

"My brother is a brute, sir, and will stop at nothing to get his own way," Letty said, enjoying herself hugely, and triumphing in a chance to get her own back at Sheldon for his high-handed using of *her*, even if he was not present to hear. "He will doubtless divert the river across your meadow stealthily by night, and shoot at anyone who dares to try and stop him."

"Oh dear, I had no notion he would go to *such* lengths," Mr Throckmorton murmured worriedly.

"Oh, without a doubt," Letty said with secret glee. "I could tell you of other occasions when — "

"No, I beg you will not, ma'am, I have heard enough. I am only thankful you have warned me."

"You are not going to cry off?" she asked sharply.

"Indeed, no, my lady," he hastened to assure her. "You have merely strengthened my resolve to stand out against Lord Langton's evil schemes."

Letty nearly choked on a suppressed

giggle at such pomposity, but she managed to keep a straight face as she said: "I am mighty glad to hear it, sir. I would there were a few more like you about to put my brother in his place properly. Tell me, what shall you do, pray?" she ended confidentially, dropping gracefully down on a green velvet sofa and looking up at him impishly.

"As to that, ma'am, I have no very clear notion as yet, but rest assured I shall think of something."

"For a start you could keep guard on your meadow, set your dogs on any trespassers, something of that nature."

"Nothing so dramatic, I trust, will be necessary, ma'am, but as a last resort — Well, let us hope it will not come to that."

"You must fight for the rights of the poor and oppressed against the tyranny of the lord of the manor," she told him. "My brother *is* tyrannical, you know, sir. You can have no notion. What I should not give to be free of him, but he is my guardian, you see, till I come of age. I am positively miserable at times."

"I have every sympathy for you,

ma'am," Mr Throckmorton said feelingly. "You must be amazingly tolerant."

"Oh, yes," she sighed dramatically, "in my position one has to be." She did not mention how tolerant in turn her brother had to be, how only the other day she had tipped her breakfast into his unsuspecting lap for reprimanding her for being saucy to a footman. But Mr Throckmorton was very gullible where women were concerned, besides he had little experience of them, and he was completely taken in by the charming young creature.

"My poor dear young lady," he murmured, flattered by her confidences. "How exceedingly dreadful for you. Does he beat you, and lock you up, and feed you on bread and water if you do not obey him implicitly?"

Such a notion almost made Letty collapse with mirth again. No doubt Sheldon would like to do all those things to her if only he had the chance. But she didn't want the Rector questioning her too closely on her private life, so she dismissed the matter by saying with an air of martyrdom: "Oh, it is surprising what one can get accustomed to."

"Yes, but — " Mr Throckmorton protested.

He got no further. At that precise moment the great double doors under their massive stone pedimant were flung open, and Lord Langton strode furiously into the room. His face was dark with temper, so that even Letty shrank back a little in dismay. He grabbed hold of her roughly and unceremoniously flung her to one side as he faced Mr Throckmorton.

"How dare you come here, sir, making up to my sister behind my back?" he cried angrily. "Get out of my house at once before I have you flung out."

He made a menacing movement towards the younger man, who stepped back hastily and nearly tripped over a chair behind him. Recovering his balance and his dignity, he stood his ground and said boldly: "I beg your pardon, my lord, but I am not making up to your sister, and that was not my reason for coming here. I came for the express purpose of seeing your lordship."

"A likely tale, by God!" the Marquis stormed. "You can have nothing to say to me. Now, out, you impudent young whippersnapper. Go dance attendance on other men's sisters."

"At least, sir," Simon was stung into defending himself, very unwisely, "I do not dance attendance on other men's wives."

The Marquis was livid with rage. He would have struck the Rector, had not Letty quickly interposed herself between them.

"Get out of my way, girl," Sheldon cried furiously.

"Would you strike a woman?" Mr Throckmorton demanded, now also roused to anger, nevertheless wisely stepping back a bit. "For shame, sir! Have you not used her ladyship ill enough already?"

Sheldon was so taken aback that his fury suddenly deserted him, and he was left staring at his unwelcome visitor blankly.

"Furthermore, my lord," Mr Throckmorton took the opportunity to say during this unusual occurrence of his lordship being lost for words, "I will stop at nothing to safeguard the rights of the villagers against your tyranny."

"Out!" Sheldon stormed, giving the reverend gentleman a kick up the reverend behind. "I'll flood the whole confounded place if I wish, aye, and cut off the water supply, too, and you won't be able to stop me. I'll teach you not to cross me again, young man."

Mr Throckmorton stumbled, nearly fell flat on his face, then miraculously saved himself from falling by clutching hold of a chairback.

"Oh, I'm so sorry, sir — " Letty began in genuine dismay, rushing to his side.

"It doesn't signify, ma'am," Simon said stoically, thinking that any indignity was worth suffering if it won him such real concern from such a fine pair of dark brown eyes. "Pray do not distress yourself. I am in no way hurt, only perhaps my pride, and what is that, when all's said and done?" Seeing that Lord Langton was about to lose his temper again, he made a curt little bow, bid brother and sister good-day, and walked quickly from the room.

Letty turned on her her brother in fury.

"How *could* you, Sheldon?" she cried

accusingly. "And to the Rector, of all people! Are you quite lost to all sense of civility? You have the temper and manners of an *oaf*!"

"And you should know better than to flirt with a man of the Church," he retorted harshly. "How dare you bring that fellow into my house without even asking my permission?"

"I did *not* bring him in," Letty shouted back at him. "He just came here asking for you, so as you weren't here I thought *I* might be able to help him. That is all, honestly, Sheldon," she ended more quietly, almost cajolingly.

"Humph!" Lord Langton grunted, not fully convinced.

"And really, you should not lose your temper like that," she went on reprovingly, "and say such dreadful things, when you have quite got the wrong end of the stick, in any event. It really is too *bad* in you, Sheldon. I was ready to sink."

"Well, I am sorry for it," Sheldon conceded, though not very graciously. "But when I learned that that preaching, prosing — *ass* was closeted with you — Well, I just flew off the handle. If it was me he really wanted to see, what the *devil* did he want, I wonder?"

The Rev. Mr Throckmorton, meanwhile, riding slowly away from Lyng House, was wondering what on earth had made him go there in the first place. He had achieved nothing, in fact, he had made a right mess of things, and was far worse off than before. And yet, somehow, it had all been worth while. To find favour with such a charming young lady as Lady Letitia Howard was worth anything, he thought.

3

EARLIER that morning, before his unfortunate encounter with the Rector, Sheldon, restless as usual, had risen early as was his wont and ridden over to Roselands, for the express purpose of acquainting Mrs Montagu with his meeting with Captain Fenner-Smith. To his surprise and fury, he had been politely but firmly informed that the mistress was incommoded and not receiving any visitors. But he had refused to be fobbed off with that, to be treated like a grubby schoolboy stealing apples, as he put it. He had insisted on seeing Mr Montagu, but the latter had been most unaccommodating, and eventually Sheldon had gone away in a rage, having delivered his message for Mrs Montagu. The knowledge that the old fellow was cutting up awkward about his affair with Josephine hardly surprised him, but it made him more determined than ever to keep Josephine for his mistress while it suited him. No country squire was going to cross him.

He was still in no very good temper when he reached home only to be informed that the Rev. Mr Throckmorton was closeted with his sister. The ensuing little scene in no way improved his dark mood. Time hung heavy on his hands. He retired to his library, two or three faithful dogs at his heels, and sat in gloomy solitude to consider his problems.

Of course, he should have known that sooner or later Montagu would cut up rough about his affair with Josephine. They had long since ceased to make any secret of it, to be at all discreet. The whole neighbourhood knew. Letty made sure of that. Well, it was not the first time he had found himself the recipient of an outraged husband's wrath. Once, even, it had come to a duel. He automatically raised a finger to the scar on his cheek as he recalled the event. Why the devil did he always play with fire? In part, it added to the excitement, of course, and in many ways a married woman was more convenient, less costly. But something inside him always drove him to flout convention, to fly in the face of public opinion. He derived much satisfaction from the outrage he caused. In a way, he concluded, he was as bad as Letty. Only with him, he knew, he was paying other people out for the hurt Amelia had once dealt him.

But that didn't solve the problem of Montagu. The damnable thing was, he quite liked the fellow, though of course he was a fool not to have put his foot down with Josephine years ago. No man should make free with *his* wife, if he ever had one, which was doubtful now. He disliked and mistrusted women intensely.

His reflections were rudely cut short by Letty's flouncing into the room to announce that she meant to go to church that morning.

"I absolutely forbid it," Sheldon said at once. "I know what you are at: running after our precious Rector, making sheep's eyes at him. Oh, no, Letty, you go too far this time."

"Good gracious, would you now keep me from worship?" Letty taunted. "For shame, brother! Even you cannot be such

70

a hardened profligate as to forbid me the blessing of holy church. Whatever would my sisters say if they knew?"

Sheldon spread his hands helplessly. "There you have me, Letty," he said in despairing tones. "I cannot, in truth, deny your attending divine service, even if you go for entirely the wrong reason. D'you know, you'll be the death of me? I'm at my wits' end with you."

She had been about to fling triumphantly out of the room, but at his last words she pulled up short and turned to look at him in surprise.

"You do but fun, Sheldon," she said, adding uncertainly: "Don't you?"

By his puckered brow she knew that he did not. In a sudden gesture of sisterly affection she went back and put her arms round him.

"I promise I will be the soul of discretion," she said earnestly. "And indeed I am very sorry to be such a sore trial to you, but when you are always so *stern*, and out of temper with me, and — Oh, well, you put my back up so you *make* me want to hurt you and defy you. And you know what a hasty temper I have, quite as bad as your own. I will be *very* good, and won't ogle Mr Throckmorton once, or put him out of countenance at all. He is really rather sweet, you know, and quite shy."

Sheldon raised a quizzical eyebrow at her.

"Indeed?" he remarked, with a faint smile.

"Oh, yes! And — and I wish you will come with me, Sheldon. Please! It will look so odd if I go alone. Everyone will stare so. And you have not been to church once since our new Rector came."

"They will stare even more if I go," he returned drily. "The Reverend gentleman will have a fit."

"Oh, yes! What famous fun!" she gurgled. "I promise to be good for a week if only you will come. *Please*, Sheldon. Only you will have to make haste if you do, else we shall be late. Oh, lord, what a stir it will cause!"

Sheldon considered, a rather vengeful, ill-natured expression on his face as he did so. It would serve Throckmorton right for Letty to lead him a merry dance, teach him that he couldn't play with fire without getting his fingers burnt. It would also give himself the chance to cut the impertinent fellow publicly. Besides, no doubt the family from Roselands would be there. He would be able to make Montagu look a fool in front of all his neighbours and underlings. He'd soon learn not to cross the Marquis of Langton.

"Very well," Sheldon said at length.

Lyng church stood, flint and old and lonely, with a recently added square tower, in its churchyard in the midst of Lyng House Park, not far from the main gates, and slightly off to the right of the long gravelled drive. To get to it, everyone had to pass through the great white gates and cross Lord Langton's land. On this particular Sunday in March, the congregation, which was quite large, was amazed by the sight of Lady Letitia Howard and her brother entering the church and making their way to the Lyng House pew. Her ladyship bobbed her bright pretty head at people as if she attended church regularly, but his lordship passed by as if no one was there, obviously despising them all, his ill nature set strongly upon his dark features. Only by the Roselands pew did he pause very deliberately, mark out Mrs Montagu for his particular attention by nodding and smiling at her briefly, then moving on to his own seat, much to the shocked outrage of the assembled company and Mr Montagu in particular. The gasp that went up could be heard almost all round the ancient building.

"Sheldon, how could you?" Letty hissed, once in the comparative privacy of the high box pew. "You made *me* promise to be on my best behaviour. Oh, how I had much rather have come with my maid!"

"If you are going to make a piece of work about it," Sheldon snapped back in an undertone, "I shall take you straight home again."

"Oh, unfair!" Letty began.

"Be quiet! Here comes your precious Mr Throckmorton."

Letty subsided into silence, and tried to put on a bright smile. Her brother lolled back in his seat, his eyes half closed, an expression of the utmost boredom on his face. Mr Throckmorton, entering his pulpit, was greatly disconcerted to see the Howard brother and sister amongst his congregation. The shock was so great he almost fell down the pulpit steps. As it was, he dropped his sermon notes on the floor. Hurriedly he bent to retrieve them with suddenly nerveless fingers, his face a fiery red. He could almost feel Lord Langton's derision. But glancing in that direction, it was Lady Letitia's sympathetic smile he caught, and all at once he felt on top of the world. It was a feeling that lasted till halfway through his sermon. He was glad he had chosen for his subject that it was easier for a camel to pass through the eye of a needle than for a rich man to enter the kingdom of heaven. It seemed so appropriate. It might almost have been written solely for Lord Langton's benefit.

Mr Throckmorton warmed to his subject, getting rather carried away, saying that at a time of national crisis, when only last week the Bank of England and all the town and country banks had stopped payment of cash on the issuing of an Order in Council by Mr Pitt, it was a sign of the callous wickedness of the rich that certain of their number could still wantonly waste money on the furtherance of their own pleasure, even to the detriment of the less well-off.

It was almost a direct hit at Lord Langton. A faint murmur went round the church, and several heads turned in the direction of the Howard pew. To the Rector's chagrin and everyone else's amusement loud snores were the only reaction from the Marquis. He was seemingly fast asleep.

It was too much for the Rev. Mr Throckmorton. He lost his train of thought, his flow of eloquence faltered, he stuttered and stumbled over his words, blushed in annoyance and confusion, and brought his sermon to a hasty conclusion. A stir went round the church. Some of the younger, more ignorant members of the congregation sniggered, older ones frowned in disapproval, some looked frankly shocked, others apprehensive. Surely their young Rector had gone too far in abusing Lord Langton. There must come reaction from one noted for his short temper and vengeful nature. But as everyone rose for the last hymn, the Marquis merely opened his eyes, glanced about him in slightly surprised contempt, got to his feet in leisurely fashion, and began to sing unconcernedly in his rich, melodious baritone.

To the relief of all, the service finally ended, and the congregation filed out in dribs and drabs into the sprightly March day. The Rector stood chatting to his flock, a little uneasily, for he was only too aware he had yet to face Lord Langton, and doubtless then the storm would break about his head.

But Sheldon was in no hurry to leave. He had not been in the church for some time, and he was shocked to notice how decayed it had become, apart from the tower. There was damp and mildew on all the walls, woodworm in the pews that had not seen a coat of varnish in years, rot in much of the woodwork, even in the floor, where in one corner a gaping hole had been cordoned off. The altar, too, was in a bad state of repair, everything about it fading and neglected.

"I declare I was ready to *sink*, Sheldon," Letty twittered at his elbow.

"You are ten times worse than I. Oh, come along, *do*! What in the world are you staring at the roof for?"

"Because unless our worthy Rector does something about it soon, he won't have a roof. Do you not observe the damp patches everywhere where the rain has been in? Indeed, the whole place is in a state of the saddest disrepair."

"What, has Mr Throckmorton's sermon born fruit with you already?" Letty jeered. "Are you to use your wealth for the benefit of others instead of merely your own pleasure?"

Her words brought Sheldon back to earth with a bump. He frowned.

"No such thing," he snapped, and strode angrily out of the church.

In the porch he came face to face with Mr Throckmorton. The two men glared at each other.

"Did you have to be quite so pointed in your remarks?" Sheldon demanded harshly.

"If the bolt went home, sir," Mr Throckmorton retorted boldly, "then it is yourself you must look to and not me."

"Self-righteous prig!" the Marquis

exclaimed in furious disgust, and strode on out into the churchyard.

"Oh dear," Letty murmured in distress, part genuine, part assumed for the young man's benefit, "I'm afraid this is all my fault. I would insist on coming to church. I had not conceived it possible of Sheldon's coming as well."

"Pray, do not be put about, my lady," Simon hastened to reassure her. "The fault in no way lies at your door. I assure you, I meant to cast no slur upon yourself. I would not so presume — "

Letty suppressed a desire to giggle. He really was the sweetest man, but a trifle pompous — Well, he could no doubt be cured of that in time.

"My brother says the roof of your church will fall in if it is not repaired soon," she said to change the subject.

Instantly she wished she had not spoken, for the Rector's face was a picture of dismay.

"He said that?" he murmured. "Oh dear, and I am persuaded he has the right of it. I had hoped it was only my imagination, but — "

"Letty!" Lord Langton shouted, striding

back into the porch. "Come along at once, will you." He stopped short at sight of the Rector's dismayed look, a thoughtful expression on his face. "Oh!" he ended in an odd tone of voice.

"I was telling Mr Throckmorton what you said about the church roof," Letty explained quickly, put out by a mood of her brother's she did not understand.

"So I understand," Sheldon returned drily. "Believe me, Throckmorton, I know what I am talking about."

"I don't doubt it, my lord," Simon said soberly, for once too troubled to be at odds with the Marquis. "I have feared it so myself ever since I came here. But what is to be done? Mine is not a rich parish." He coloured up as he realized what he was saying, being strongly minded of his own recent sermon.

"I'll tell you what," Sheldon said slowly, as if carefully weighing each word, "I'll strike a bargain with you. You let me divert the river across your meadow, and I'll engage to repair not only the church roof for you, but also the whole of the fabric."

The Rector studied the older man's

face, trying to assess the spirit in which the offer was made, whether it was a genuine offer whereby his lordship considered he was making a fair exchange, or whether it was said merely to taunt him, to score one over him, my lord knowing full well that he could never sell his parishioners' rights even for such a gain to their own benefit. But Lord Langton's dark face was inscrutable.

"I very much fear, my lord," he said at length, but regretfully, "that it is an offer I find impossible to accept."

"Well," Sheldon returned equably, "I will give you a few days to think on it, for I assure you it is an offer not lightly made, and as such I do not think you can afford to lightly reject it out of hand. So consider it, sir, and I will ask you again in a few days' time what decision you arrive at. Good-day to you."

Much perplexed, Mr Throckmorton stood gazing after Lord Langton's tall, broad figure as he walked away.

★ ★ ★

Somewhere among the maze of twisting Norfolk lanes, on their way to New Lyng, Rosalind Fenner-Smith and her mother had got lost, and ended up in King's Lynn, a fine old port situated on the Great Ouse at the southern end of the Wash. By the time they were once more on the right road, and nearing their destination, the day was far spent, the bright spring sunshine fast fading to dusk, and they were tired, hungry and dispirited. Now that they were actually about to come face to face with Captain Michael Fenner-Smith, who was practically a stranger to them, the task did not seem so easy. What would he be like after so long? How would he receive them? How would he take the news of his brother's death and his own new status as Sir Philip's heir?

They turned left off the main Lynn-Fakenham road, and were soon in what appeared to be a broad avenue of trees that suddenly plunged downhill and they were in the orderly model village street of New Lyng, dominated by the great ornate white gates of Lyng House at the bottom. They descended the slope, and then, where the road split to right and left before those gates, they came to a halt, uncertain where to go next.

"Shall I enquire at the lodge, ma'am?" the coachman opened the door to ask.

"Yes, I think that will be quite the best thing, Tomkins," Mrs Fenner-Smith said decidedly. "Else we shall be driving round for an age, and it is near dark already."

"Very good, ma'am."

However, the coachman was saved the bother, for at that moment a lone horseman came along the road, and seeing the carriage drawn up uncertainly, drew rein and addressed the coachman.

"Can I be of assistance to you? Are you gone out of your way?" a very cultured but rather abrupt voice asked.

Rosalind let down the window to answer the speaker. In the gathering gloom she saw, astride a large dark horse, a large dark man, rather well-looking were it not for his discontented expression.

"We are seeking a house called Long Croft," she replied politely. "If of your kindness you could but direct us there. I fear we may have missed it."

"Indeed you have," the man informed her, unable to keep some of the surprise out of his voice. "I have just come from there myself."

It was Rosalind's turn to be surprised. What could this autocratic gentleman be doing with Uncle Michael? But then she remembered that she really knew nothing of her uncle.

"You are perhaps acquainted with my uncle, sir," she said, "Captain Michael Fenner-Smith."

At that the man drew nearer, and peered at her in a way that would doubtless have made a lesser female cringe. It was as if he were weighing her up, expecting to find fault with her. She felt some annoyance. She knew she was no oil painting, but to be scrutinized in that ill-natured manner — Well, she would soon stare him out of countenance.

To her astonishment the gentleman only laughed a little self-consciously.

"I beg your pardon, ma'am," he apologized. "I did not mean to stare so at you. Most remiss of me. But I must confess to being all amazement at meeting you. I had not known the Captain had a niece. You see," he hurried on to explain, as she still continued to stare at him, "I am quite well acquainted with him, and he never mentioned that he had any relatives other than a father and brother."

"That is because he has not seen us for over a dozen years," Rosalind told him, kindly lowering her unnerving gaze to set him at ease again. "He has no notion we are come. I am Rosalind Fenner-Smith. His brother was my father."

"Was?" the gentleman said quickly. "Is he — "

"He was killed at Cape St Vincent," she said quietly. "That is why we are here, my mother and I, to break the news to my uncle." She stopped short, realizing she was telling all this to a complete stranger. Her stupid tongue always did run away with her. But if this man was really a friend of Uncle Michael's, what harm?

"I am sorry for it," the gentleman was saying, though with no softening of his abrupt manner. "Doubtless it will come as a great shock to him. I trust it will not overset him too much."

"Overset him?" she queried in some bewilderment. "It is bound to, is it not?"

"Yes, of course, ma'am, but I do not think you fully comprehend." The abrupt tone was growing perceptibly if slightly impatient. "Your uncle lives almost like a recluse, for one thing. He has practically shut himself away from the world. He suffers much from an old wound in the leg, and — "

"Are you his doctor, pray?" Rosalind asked, not really thinking such a supercilious gentleman could be anything near so commonplace, but she could not imagine what else such a one should have to do with the image she was building up of her uncle.

To her complete astonishment, the stranger gave a loud hoot of laughter.

"I, a doctor?" he cried. "Good God, ma'am, you do me too much honour. I am the last one to be called to such a profession."

"Oh, I beg your pardon, sir," Rosalind said in some confusion. "How very uncivil in me, to be sure. I had not meant — "

"Pray do not regard it. But let me not detain you. You have already passed Long Croft. It is that thatched monstrosity at the end of the street, on your right going back."

"That thatched *what*?" Rosalind queried, not sure if she had heard aright.

"Cottage, I should say," the man corrected himself. "Only I find it in the most execrable taste. It is wholly out of place in New Lyng. Now, I must bid you good-evening. I shall wait upon your uncle in the morning to offer my condolences. You may tell him you met Lord Langton in your way here. Your servant, ma'am."

He dug his spurs into his horse's sides and rode sharply away, without even raising his hat.

"Oh dear, and I thought he was the doctor," Rosalind exclaimed ruefully as she sat back beside her mother. "What a dreadful mistake to make. He must live in the big house beyond those huge gates. Trust me to put my foot in it!"

"Never mind, dear, he seemed to think it a huge joke," Mrs Fenner-Smith consoled her. "Only fancy your Uncle

Michael having such a fine gentleman for his friend."

"He did not say he was a friend, precisely, only an acquaintance. I hope we may not see too much of him. I did not care for him overmuch. A cold, hard man. Such an impatient way of speaking, and such a discontented expression."

"Well, I dare say he cannot help that, my love. But let us not trouble ourselves about him. We have my poor brother-in-law to concern ourselves with."

A few minutes later the carriage was churning up the muddy track through the trees to the yard at the back of Captain Fenner-Smith's ornate gothic cottage. In some trepidation they climbed down from the vehicle, and groped their way round to the front door. For what seemed a long time they stood shivering in the chilly evening air. The tall trees rustled eerily above and all around them. The house seemed to be in darkness, and for a moment they wondered if their relative had gone to bed. But at long last the door opened, and a tall, lean man stood there holding aloft a flickering lantern.

"Yes?" he said a little uncertainly.

"Who are you, pray?"

"Captain Fenner-Smith?" Mrs Fenner-Smith asked, stepping forward. He had aged so much, changed so much, she hardly recognized him. Even now, she was not sure.

"Yes," he replied, his eyes narrowing as he looked hard at her.

"I am Liza, your sister-in-law. Do you not recollect me?"

"Liza? I scarce recall. Liza! My brother's wife?"

"Yes, yes, the same. And this is my daughter Rosalind, your niece. She was a schoolgirl when last you set eyes on her. We have just come from your father, Sir Philip."

"Good heaven! It can't be, after all these years. But I see it is." The Captain was plainly much overcome. "What brings you here after so long, and at this time of night?"

"We lost our way and ended up in King's Lynn. But may we not come in? Your father's carriage is without."

"Do you propose staying? I am hardly in a position to put you up. I do not entertain visitors. I live quite alone, with only a daily woman who comes in from the village."

"No matter," Rosalind said decidedly. She had had enough of standing on the doorstep, after coming so many miles. She took a resolute step towards her uncle, who automatically moved aside to let her by. "We shall cope excessively well, I am persuaded. Mama and I can do all that has to be done."

"Pray, do come in," the Captain said, trying to collect himself. "Of course, you are most welcome. But why are you come?"

The poor man did indeed seem quite bewildered. Bearing in mind the words of the large, dark man called Lord Langton, Rosalind's attitude softened.

"Let Mama come and talk to you while I deal with the coachman. Have you stables, sir, or an outhouse?"

"I keep no carriage or horse, I do not need one, but yes, I have an outhouse of sorts. A friend of mine stables his horse there sometimes. You will find what you need, I trust. And your coachman may bed down in the room over the outhouse."

"Thank you, sir. I shall manage."

Rosalind went off to deal with the carriage, leaving her mother to face the Captain and break the news to him of his brother's death and what it meant in the way of his altered status.

4

FOR several days after that memorable service in Lyng church, Lord Langton was in an even more morose, restless, frustrated mood than before. For one thing, the matter of the Rector's meadow stood at temporary stalemate while he gave the Rev. Mr Throckmorton time to reconsider his proposal about repairing the church. While that was in the offing, he did not want to go ahead and broach Crazy Mick about diverting the river across Long Croft land. For another, Letty had suddenly started behaving oddly. Ever since that Sunday she had been a model of decorum, had only let fly at him twice, had only thrown her slipper at him once, and, most important of all, had not abused him or taunted him once. He was deeply disturbed about her, and wondered what she could be at. Finally, there was the problem of Josephine. She had not been near him since she had come to tell him about Crazy Mick. All he had had from her was a brief little note to say that she was a trifle unwell, and trusted she did not incommode him too much. Remembering that other time when she was breeding, a great uneasiness descended upon him. Soon, he felt sure, the storm was going to break about his head. It was the last thing he wanted at present, especially with her husband starting to cut up awkward over their affair.

The only good to come out of those depressing days, he thought, was his growing friendship with Michael Fenner-Smith. For some unknown reason the village recluse seemed to have taken a liking to him, though he had to admit in all honesty, ill-assorted couple that they were, he felt the same about the Captain. He had few friends, certainly none in the immediate neighbourhood, for people did not take to him easily, any more than he did to them. But between him and Crazy Mick there was an affinity, an understanding, born of a complete lack of humbug on either side. Every day, at the Captain's request, he rode over to Long Croft, there to sit in perfect male bliss, uncluttered by any females, drinking, smoking, playing cards, talking, but most of all discussing their mutual interest of gardening.

It was when returning from one such jaunt late one evening that he first met the Captain's niece.

As the carriage of the female Fenner-Smiths vanished up the road, Sheldon rode slowly and thoughtfully back to Lyng House. It had come as rather a surprise to him to learn that his friend had a niece and a sister-in-law, for he had never spoken of them. But then, he reflected, a man might have his reasons for not mentioning his family. He himself rarely spoke of Amelia. She was a part of his life he wanted to forget. Likewise, was there some reason why the Captain never talked of his brother's family? As for the brother's death at Cape St Vincent, well, he, Sheldon, was really sorry for it for his friend's sake. It brought the war, which he usually managed to ignore, so much nearer home. First thing in the morning he must go to Long Croft and offer his condolences. Somehow he felt oddly responsible for the Captain's well-being.

Sheldon went early to bed that night, awaking in a cold sweat early next morning to find that he had been dreaming of Amelia, that she had come back after twelve long years to torment him. Consequently he was in an even worse mood than usual when he went down to breakfast, a mood that was in no way lightened by the sight of Letty already sitting at table devouring mouthfuls of toast and marmalade.

"For God's sake, you're about early, aren't you?" he said irritably, as he sat down opposite her.

"So are you," she retorted in an unladylike manner, her mouth full.

"For heaven's sake, girl," he exclaimed bad-temperedly, "cannot you mind your manners once in a while? You eat like a pig. Cannot you conduct yourself like a lady?"

"The fault is all yours," she retorted saucily. "You brought me up. Therefore my manners must be a reflection of your own."

Realizing he was fighting a losing battle, and that if he was not careful he would get her toast and marmalade in his face, he bit back the angry retort that rose to his lips, and shrugged helplessly.

"I must confess, I know not what to do with you, Letty," he said despairingly. "Nothing I can say or do is right. You rip me up at every turn. What in the world am I to do with you?"

"Let me go to London," she said eagerly. "Only pray do, Sheldon. You may take me. The season starts soon. I promise you I would make a brilliant match there, and then you would never be bothered with me again. *Why* will you not let me go, Sheldon? Just because you once got jilted by that odious female, what's-her-name — Amelia Somebody-or-other — "

"*Hold* your tongue, Letty!" he cried in more hurt than anger.

"Why?" Letty pursued relentlessly. "Everyone knows she threw you over for a mere half-pay Navy officer, because you were so *odious* and *selfish* she could not bear the thought of marrying you. Is that not so?"

Sheldon stirred his coffee vigorously before answering, trying to give himself time to overcome the ache in his heart. After all this time even mention of her name was like a knife in the wound. He didn't know how much longer he could stand Letty's cruel taunts.

"Letty, please," he said placatingly, as he always did when he thought he had gone too far with her. "Let us not drag up the past. I promise I will take you to London, in a few weeks' time. Only — " He paused, staring at her helplessly.

"Only?" she prompted, adding unkindly: "Only you cannot leave Mrs Montagu."

"*No!*" he cried in vexation. "Nothing of the sort. Josephine does not come into it. I want only to do what is best for you, Letty. I must confess, I have failed to bring you up as my parents could have wished, but I have done my best. It has not been easy. I have not known how to go on with you always. I have had to be both mother and father to you, and I have failed miserably. The trouble is, my dear, I am over fond of you. I have tried to give you everything, and I have not wanted to hurt you at all."

"Pooh!" her ladyship said rudely. "You are nothing but an overbearing tyrant, and you have been more like a jailer than a loving brother. All you care for is yourself. It is small wonder even Mrs Montagu does not come near you now."

"Be quiet, girl!" he shouted angrily, starting up.

"*Pooh!*" Letty said again, very rudely and very emphatically, and, getting up, threw the sugar bowl at him and rushed from the room.

Sheldon sat down again, heavy hearted and in despair, and absently began brushing the sugar off his clothes. The bowl had fortunately fallen wide, only catching him on the knuckles before smashing on the carpet beyond. He sucked his sore knuckles, and discovered that one was bleeding. What *on earth*, he wondered, did a man do with such a sister? He supposed he should have been firmer with her, but she was the one person he could not use so. With everyone else he was ruthless, but with Letty, he was completely at her mercy. He could hardly understand it himself, the effect she had on him. Perhaps it was because he was so fond of her, felt so responsible for her. It was ironic, he reflected sadly, how those he really cared for responded by hating him and hurting him. So it had been with Amelia.

Nevertheless, he ate a hearty breakfast, for he was a big man and had a good appetite never impaired by over-indulgence or ill health. He took plenty of strenuous exercise, went for a hard ride every day to keep himself in good trim, and had frequent cold baths.

As soon as he had finished eating, only pausing to issue sharp orders to the attendant footman to clear up the mess of sugar, he went straight to the stables and had the grey mare saddled.

On his way across the park, he went out of his way to look at the church. Now it had come to his notice, he was only too aware of its state of dereliction, and it depressed him immeasurably. He ought to have set repairs in motion at once, but in a moment of pique he had made it an issue in his battle with the Rector, and now how he wished the devil he had not. If Throckmorton rejected his proposal, as he was beginning to feel sure he would, the church would be in real danger of falling into complete decay, for the parish was not a rich one. The loss of such an ancient, beautiful building was not to be contemplated. Perhaps, for just once in his life, he should climb down, eat humble pie, go and see Throckmorton, and put a new proposal to him: that he, Langton, have the church repaired unconditionally.

He smiled rather cynically to himself. The Marquis of Langton making a turnabout! Such a thing was unheard of. He must be getting soft in his old age. Had not Josephine recently said something about his getting senile? At thought of her, his habitual frown descended on his brow again, and in morose mood he rode off to Long Croft.

As had become his habit, he rode up to the back of the house, and stabled his horse in the outhouse. He was surprised to see the ancient travelling carriage and horses there, for he had momentarily forgotten the existence of the Captain's female relatives. Well, he would not stop long today, so he would not inconvenience them too much.

Unlike his usual practice, he went round to the front door, and politely knocked. Eventually Crazy Mick himself, looking rather hollow-eyed, came to answer the door. His tired expression brightened at sight of his visitor.

"Ah, Langton, my dear friend, how happy I am to see you at a time like this. Pray come in."

"Believe me, I am prodigious sorry to hear of your loss, Smith," Sheldon said abruptly, never any good at expressing deep emotion. It was one of the unfortunate reasons why he was always taken to be such a cold, heartless fellow.

"Thank you, yes, it was a great shock, though I suppose it should not have been." The Captain spoke rather vaguely, as if the shock had somewhat impaired his powers of thought.

Sheldon looked at him anxiously. He suspected that it would not take much to overset his friend completely and send him out of his mind. What else besides the death of his brother had happened to disturb him so greatly? Was it the sudden appearance after so long of his niece and sister-in-law.

"I will not impose myself upon you at a time like this, sir," he said, "but I felt I must offer my condolences."

"No, pray do not go, Langton," the Captain begged. "The ladies are within. I believe you met them and directed them here last night. Will you not partake of a glass of madeira with them?"

Sheldon hesitated. He was in no mood for social chitchat, and the presence of strangers, females at that, meant he could not converse with Captain Fenner-Smith in their usual free-and-easy manner.

"You need not mind my sister-in-law and niece," the Captain said, as if reading the Marquis's mind. "They are both very broad-minded. I wish to talk to you, my friend, ask your advice. Come in, I beg of you."

"Very well," Sheldon said, his manner as stiff and abrupt as ever, though at heart he was deeply touched by his friend's request.

Rosalind, hearing his voice from the parlour, thought what an unfeeling, self-opinionated man he was. She had no wish to have to sit and talk to him. She was bound to say something to put him out of countenance, and that would upset Uncle Michael. Oh dear, what a trial the wretched man was going to be! Why could he not take himself off and leave them alone? She was sure he did not really care a rap for her uncle.

Sheldon, striding into the parlour, was pulled up short by the sight of Rosalind, who was nearest the door. Last night, in the half light, and with the carriage and her travelling cloak hiding most of her person, he had not been able to see her properly, indeed, he had given the matter little thought. Now, getting a full view of her, he could not help pulling up in amazement. He, who loved beautiful things and beautiful women, had never seen anything quite like Rosalind Fenner-Smith before. He was a large man, she was almost as big, but her figure was not even good, being shapeless in places and lumpy in others. She wore a black mourning dress that did nothing for her colouring, while her pale red hair flowed unfashionably right down her back to her bottom. As for her horsy face, with its prominent nose, protruding teeth, and pale blue eyes behind unflattering spectacles, well — It was past words.

Good God, he thought, and only just stopped himself exclaiming it aloud. He had never seen anyone so ugly in his life before.

But the way he had stopped short, the look on his face, was enough to convey only too clearly to Rosalind what he thought of her. The knowledge annoyed and hurt her, not that she wasn't used to such reactions to her appearance, but with this supercilious stranger, his own figure so shapely, his features so regular and comely, his clothes so obviously expensive and in such good taste, his revulsion of her was so blatant that it was like a slap round the face. It wasn't often she did not like anyone, always generously making allowances for human failings, but this man she disliked at once.

Sheldon hastily recollected himself, ashamed of his momentary display of bad manners. He detested above all things ill-breeding in people. And anyway, was he not always saying that looks are deceptive? In all probability the young woman had a beautiful character. So he managed to smile faintly at her, saying politely: "Your servant, ma'am," adding to the older woman whom he had hardly noticed till that moment: "And yours, too, ma'am."

"Lord Langton is a close friend of mine," the Captain was saying, "though we have our differences of opinion."

Rosalind could not imagine anyone being allowed to have a difference of opinion with his lordship.

The ladies made their curtseys, while the Captain set out glasses and a bottle of madeira. There was an awkward little silence while he poured out the drink and handed it round. Sheldon sat down on the only vacant chair, next to that of Miss Fenner-Smith, and wondered what was coming next.

"You see, Langton," Crazy Mick said at length, as if taking up the thread of a conversation he had only just left off, "I have not seen my sister-in-law and niece for twelve or fifteen years. I misremember precisely."

"So I am given to understand by your niece," the Marquis commented non-committally.

"The thing is — " The Captain paused and took a great breath. "With the death of my brother, I am now my father's heir."

"I see." Sheldon's tone was as non-committal as ever, and Rosalind shot him a look of dislike. What an unfeeling man, to be sure!

"I know not quite what to do for the best," the older man went on worriedly. "My father will not see me, yet, though he sends me his blessing. What am I to make of it? I should go back to Hertfordshire, but I have no wish to leave Long Croft, or even Norfolk. Yet as the sole heir to Harford Grange — And again, should I eat humble pie and go back and crave my father's forgiveness?"

"I beg your pardon, Smith, but I am rather in the dark about all this," Sheldon said evenly. "You have mentioned before that you quarrelled with your father long ago, but you never told me what about. If you seriously wish me to advise you, I would know all the facts."

Such cool impertinence, Rosalind

thought indignantly. As if it was any business of his! She nearly said so. Strong drink always loosened her tongue, sometimes with disastrous consequences.

"It was a matter of my marriage, sir," the Captain explained, a little guardedly, Sheldon thought. "My father did not approve, neither of my chosen bride nor of the manner in which we wed. We — ran off together, you see."

"Yes," Lord Langton said flatly, rather coldly, thinking of Amelia. "I understand."

Of course you don't, Rosalind thought angrily. How could you? You have no heart, of that I am sure.

Feeling her eyes upon him, Sheldon half turned to her, one eyebrow raised in quizzical displeasure.

"And now," the Captain said unhappily, "I have not even heirs to show for it. Think you I should try to find my wife, or what? This sudden news has made me go all to pieces. You must help me, Langton. You are a man of the world."

That much, at least, Rosalind thought, was undoubtedly true.

Sheldon swirled the liquid round and round in his glass, regarding it steadily.

"I see your problem, Smith," he said at length. Even his term of addressing her uncle annoyed Rosalind. "But for a start I would certainly not advise you to try and find your wife. For one thing, unless you know where she is, or might be, 'twould be like looking for a needle in a haystack. For another, forgive me, but I doubt she wishes to come back to you or she would have done so, even if she is still alive. And lastly, forgive me again, even if you did find her, and had her back, surely after all these years she would be incapable of producing an heir, if that is what you had in mind."

The Captain had blushed scarlet to the tips of his ears. He mumbled self-defensively but with great embarrassment: "She was a great deal younger than I, Langton, more your own age, perhaps even less. She would be a young woman still. Such a delicate subject. Pray forgive me." He hurriedly gulped down his madeira, and nervously got up to refill his glass at once.

Odd how some men were so squeamish about such subjects, Sheldon reflected. As well they were not all so. He was nothing if not a realist. But there was unfortunately a modern tendency towards squeamishness. It went along with this passion for so-called romantic Gothic, a return to the 'innocence' of the natural world, to the pastoral delights. For himself he had no patience with it. It would produce a generation of simpering, missish young women with their heads buried in the sand, no use to anyone, and a race of hypocritical young men, who would show one face to the world, while pushing their natural failings out of sight. Such an attitude, that pretended to such prudish respectability, only drove ugliness and human wickedness underground. It did not eradicate it. Far better to have it out in the open, where it could be judged for what it was. But then, he supposed, he was rather old-fashioned, in heart and mind he belonged to an earlier generation, an ordered one that believed in reason and plain-speaking, and lived accordingly, an age that had produced beautiful classical music and architecture and art. Now everything was become a cheap sham, like this cottage he was sitting in. It was a sign of the times, of the machine-made trash that was resulting from the growing industrialisation of the country.

Carried away by his own thoughts, Lord Langton was unaware that he was frowning so darkly at his glass, so much so that Rosalind, still eyeing him with the greatest disfavour, was moved to exclaim in an undertone: "Do your thoughts disturb you so that you frown so angrily?"

"What? Oh, I beg your pardon, ma'am," he said hastily, with a faint smile. "I was but reflecting on the state of the world we live in."

"Then your conclusion must be that it is a sad, dreadful place, my lord," Rosalind responded bluntly.

"I fear so. Things move apace so and we are not equipped to cope with them."

"You mean," she cried eagerly, suddenly thinking she understood, "like the Enclosure Acts, that force so many poor country folk to leave their homes and seek work in the towns?"

"Something like that, though I must confess to my anxieties being on a far more intellectual level."

"Oh, so you care only for *intellect*, and not for human suffering?" she cried accusingly.

He was surprised at the passion in her voice, and paused to look at her steadily. Her pale eyes behind their disfiguring spectacles were alight with the same passion, there was a pink flush on her cheeks. He realized, with something of a start, that she had beautiful skin, like the soft smooth petals of a rose, and that she was not the dull pudding he had at first supposed her.

"I did not say that, ma'am," he said quietly, surprising himself even more that he had not lost his temper with anyone who dared contradict him or raise their voice to him.

"Then what are you, as a rich and privileged member of society, doing about it?" she shot at him.

"I must confess, nothing," he answered honestly.

"You seem to me to be a thinking man, and yet you do nothing. For shame, my lord — "

"Rosalind, my love, pray do not be mounting your favourite hobby horse to his lordship at this precise moment," Mrs Fenner-Smith put in gently but slightly reprovingly. "He was talking to your Uncle Michael."

The intense light died in Rosalind's eyes, and she subsided into a pudding again.

"I beg your pardon, my lord," she said flatly. "Pray forgive me. My stupid tongue runs away with me at times."

Unaccountably he felt sorry for her. He said, his tone softer and more gentle than usual: "Never mind. Perhaps we may continue our discussion another time. You and your mother must come up to Lyng House some time and meet my sister."

"Thank you, I should like that excessively," she returned, and was surprised to find that she really would.

"So you do not think I should try to find my wife, Langton?" the Captain asked.

"No," Sheldon answered shortly.

"And what of myself, my father? Should I go to him, should I give up this place?"

"Most definitely not," the Marquis

112

said decidedly. "Why humble yourself to him? He will not think any the more of you for it. When he wants to see you he will doubtless send for you. Until that time I would advise you to stay put where you are. Why, your father could even outlive you, and then, I presume, your niece will inherit everything, or is the estate entailed?"

"No, everything will one day go to Rosalind, sir, and I doubt there could be a more deserving heiress."

"I've no doubt of it," Sheldon said abruptly, getting up, suddenly feeling he was getting too involved in the private affairs of the Fenner-Smiths. After all, what were they to him beyond the liking and companionship he had for the Captain? He had enough problems of his own —

There was a sudden rap on the front door. In surprise, Crazy Mick limped to open it.

"Langton, it is for you," he exclaimed, coming back almost at once. "It is your sister."

"My God, what the devil — " Sheldon began in alarm, turning pale.

"She has had an accident, my friend. She is at the Rectory."

* * *

Lady Letitia Howard, having dramatically flung the sugar bowl at her brother and stormed out of the breakfast-room at Lyng House, rushed up to her room, shed a flood of angry tears, then, in a rebellious mood, put on her most dashing outfit, a redingote of cherry red velvet that enhanced her dark colouring, and went straight to the stable block, imperiously ordering her brother's phaeton to be hitched to his most spirited chestnuts.

"Milady, I cannot," James the head groom protested. "It is more than my life is worth. His lordship would never forgive me if I was to let you drive his phaeton, *and* with the chestnuts, without his knowledge. He'd dismiss me on the spot without a reference, and I wouldn't blame him."

"My brother is an odious tyrant, James," Letty retorted in a tone that brooked no argument. "And I am sick to death of his high-handed ways and of being kept in the country like this all the time. It is so monstrous *dull*, I declare. So pray do as I say, or it will go vastly ill with you. I shall tell his lordship such a tale of your insolence and disobedience to me that he will dismiss you, in any event."

James sighed with resignation. He knew her ladyship was quite capable of such outlandish behaviour, and that the master always heeded what she said. She was a right little mischief-maker, that one, and it was a pity Lord Langton could not see it and give her the thorough spanking she so richly deserved instead of indulging her all the time.

"Very well, milady," he agreed reluctantly. "Be it on your own head."

"It will be, never fear," she retorted gaily, happy now that she had got her own way. "I shall drive exceedingly *carefully*, and I dare say my brother will never know I have been out, unless you split on me, James."

"I shall never do that, milady," James assured her fervently, thinking he would never dare risk incurring my lord's dreadful wrath by so doing.

"Capital!" she cried in delight. "Heavens, what a lark this is, to be sure! Sheldon would be mad as fire if he knew."

"You will have a care, won't you, milady? These chestnuts are in rare high fettle — "

"Of course I'll have a care. It's not as if I can't drive."

James wisely said nothing, and went disapprovingly about his task. The smart phaeton was led out, and the Marquis's prize chestnuts harnessed to it. Letty, with a defiant, triumphant air, climbed up and took the ribbons. She was a little annoyed when James himself got up behind.

"There is not the least need for *you* to come with me, James," she said crossly. "One of the boys will do as well."

"I'm coming with you or you don't go, milady," James said stolidly, and refused to be budged, even on pain of dismissal.

So a few minutes later, Letty drove the high-stepping pair carefully out of the stable-yard, with the head groom, no less, up behind her in her brother's spanking turn-out. She took the back drive that came out opposite the Rectory. As she gained the open park, she gathered confidence and increased her speed, the thrill of her little venture rather going to her head. She would sweep past the Rectory, hoping Mr Throckmorton might see her so that she could impress him with her skill.

The March wind stung her cheeks and whipped up her blood. She felt wild and free at last, free of all restraint imposed by her tyrannical brother. Her mood grew even more reckless. She was obsessed with her own skill and daring, her power over the chestnuts and the vehicle. She took the bend into the lane at a great rate. The phaeton began to rock wildly. James shouted a warning. Too late she tried to avoid the gatepost. She swerved but not in time. She screamed frantically. The horses panicked, the nearside wheel hit the post with a sickening crash, overturning the carriage and throwing Letty into the stony roadway. Her head hit a large flint, and she lay unconscious in the lane with the blood seeping into her hair.

The Rev. Mr Simon Throckmorton, pottering contentedly about his garden, was looking to see if Timothy the tortoise, bequeathed him by his predecessor, had yet stirred from his winter sleep by the wall where the peach tree grew, when he heard Letty's scream followed immediately by the crash. Forgetting all about Timothy, he rushed out into the lane, only to pull up in horror at what he saw there: Lady Letitia Howard lying limp in the road, the groom staggering about dazedly, the wrecked overturned vehicle, and the panic-stricken horses entangled in the reins.

"My God!" Mr Throckmorton exclaimed, and went racing off to find his house-keeper Mrs Craske, his man-servant Henry, and his odd-job man Jonas.

Mr Throckmorton himself carefully carried Letty into the Rectory, where she was laid out on the guest room bed while Mrs Craske fussed round her, Henry was sent for the doctor, and the Rector and Jonas went to see what was to be done with the wreckage. James, recovering somewhat, was tending to the horses. It was only some time later, when Letty lay between snowy lavender-scented sheets, and the doctor arrived to pronounce that she was badly concussed and must not be moved, that anyone thought of letting Lord Langton know of the accident. They all stood staring at each other in dismay, each only too aware of his lordship's nasty, unreasonable temper. What on earth would he say — or do?

"Of course, he must be told," the Rector said firmly, and decided that Jonas should be sent to Lyng House with a message.

★ ★ ★

Sheldon's alarm for Letty, as soon as he heard that she was at the Rectory, turned to fury.

"What the deuce is she doing *there*?" he demanded violently.

"You'm best be coming, m'lud," Jonas murmured unhappily from the front door, twisting his hat round and round in his hands.

"And do you always encourage servants to use the front door, Smith?" the Marquis demanded angrily and quite unreasonably. "It is in excessively bad form, you know."

"No one can ever find the back door," the Captain mumbled, quite overcome at the sudden turn of events and in particular by this display of temper in his friend.

"Don't you think, my lord," Rosalind said loudly in her downright way, "that you should be worrying more about your sister and less about the niceties of etiquette? She may be seriously hurt. You have not even bothered to enquire."

She had stood up, and was so tall she could almost look him directly in the eyes. There was a fierce sparkle in her gaze, a spot of colour in her cheeks. Sheldon was so taken aback his own temper cooled somewhat. He glowered back at her for a moment, and then said abruptly:

"Of course. You are right. I beg your pardon."

He turned sharply away from her, nodded curtly at Mrs Fenner-Smith, picked up his hat, gloves and whip, and made to go, saying briefly if more gently to the Captain: "Forgive me, Smith, I am in a foul temper at present, and in no mood for pleasantries. Good-day to you, my friend. Good-day, ladies."

He had reached his horse before Miss Fenner-Smith came running after him, a cloak flying about her shoulders, holding her hideous skirts aloft in a most unladylike manner as she did so.

"A moment, my lord," she said a little breathlessly.

"Pray do not delay me, Miss Smith," he said impatiently. "Cannot you see I am in a hurry?"

"I think I ought to come with you, my lord," Rosalind announced in a determined tone that brooked no argument. "If your sister is injured, in a strange house, you have no female with you. Have you not thought," she added with an unmistakable taunt in her voice, "how unseemly 'twould be for a gentleman to tend to such matters alone?"

"Damn you, Miss Smith!" he exclaimed savagely. "This is none of your business.

Go and do your good works elsewhere where they are needed."

She coloured up at that, for once hurt by his words, but she rallied at once. Anyone that called her plain 'Miss Smith' in such a contemptuous way was not going to get the better of her.

"Your sister, sir," she said bluntly, "may need nursing. Are you any good at nursing?"

He regarded her steadily, trying to get a grip on his temper.

"I doubt it," he replied at length, ungraciously. He added sarcastically: "Are you proposing to share my horse with me, pray?"

"Yes," she answered at once.

He gave a sudden shout of laughter, the way he had done the night before and so much surprised her.

"Good God, Miss Smith, what a curst rum one you are, to be sure," he cried. "First you ask me if I am a doctor, now you calmly inform me you design mounting my horse with me. Conceive of it! We are neither of us precisely small."

His laughter confused her as much as anything.

"I beg your pardon, my lord," she said. "I only wanted to help."

"Come along, Miss Smith," he returned, more kindly, "up you come. Only if the animal collapses beneath us, pray do not be surprised."

Without any assistance she clambered up easily behind him and, even more to his amazement, sat astride the animal, quite unconcernedly fastening her arms round his waist to cling on. In any other female such an action would be positively *fast*, even inviting. This astonishing creature did it so matter-of-factly he could not possibly misjudge her motives. It was almost comical.

"Are you in the habit of clasping gentlemen scarce known to you about their middles, Miss Smith?" he demanded, recoiling a little from such close contact with her. "It is not really the done thing, you know."

"Oh, I beg your pardon," she said at once, in her forthright way, not taking offence at all. "Are you embarrassed by it? But it is quite the most sensible way to prevent my falling off."

"So I perceive," he commented drily,

realizing with a start that he *was* slightly embarrassed. Even Josephine did not take such liberties with his person except when they were making love. Having a strange young female suddenly grabbing him at a spot not far short of his private parts was a new experience for him.

"Well, I am sorry for it, but you will have to put up with it," she said tartly. "I cannot tolerate squeamishness."

"Nor can I," he rejoined, with a faint smile that she could not see but could detect in his voice.

They set off at a slow trot, Rosalind clinging on for dear life. It was obvious to Sheldon that she was not very at home on a horse. As they went down the village street, the habitual frown descended on his brow again. The silence became ominous. Rosalind experienced an odd sensation. She had never held men in very high esteem. Certainly one had never aroused her interest. And she had nursed far too many of them ever to be embarrassed by anything physical about them. But suddenly she was amazed to find that she liked the feel of this particular

124

man, and he was fast coming to interest her.

Sheldon was far from feeling any interest in or desire for Rosalind Fenner-Smith. He was totally engrossed in worrying about Letty, wondering what exactly had happened to her, how badly she was hurt, how the accident had occurred, and what the devil she was doing at the Rectory, of all places. It frustrated him that his pace was slowed up by the presence of the Captain's niece.

"You are really exceeding anxious for your sister, sir?" Rosalind said at length, unable to bear the grim silence any longer. "You are prodigious quiet."

"I do not believe in wasting breath on trivialities," he retorted sharply. "But yes, of course I am anxious for my sister. She is under age and my responsibility, apart from anything else. Why must you persist in minding my business for me?"

She was not at all disconcerted by this thrust.

"You know enough of mine," she answered in a rallying tone.

"Believe me, not by any design of my

125

own," he retorted crushingly.

But she was not to be crushed.

"You really are the most disagreeable man ever," she told him.

"Then if you have any sense you will keep out of my way," he returned, with growing anger.

"That I cannot at present," she said practically.

They lapsed into silence again, and this time she did not attempt to break it.

5

HIS face like a thundercloud, Lord Langton strode into the Rectory after Mrs Craske who had opened the door to him and Miss Fenner-Smith.

"Where is my sister?" he demanded harshly.

The Rector's housekeeper, who stood in the greatest awe and dislike of the Marquis, backed away from him nervously.

The Rev. Mr Throckmorton, entering the hall at that precise moment, exclaimed indignantly: "That is no way to address my housekeeper, sir."

"Damn you, Throckmorton, I want no more of your sermons. Where is my sister? What happened to her? Why the devil is she here?"

"She is upstairs in my guest chamber, my lord," Simon said calmly. "She is badly concussed, the doctor says, and must not be moved yet awhile. She has a nasty cut on the head where she fell on a sharp stone."

"Good God!" Sheldon exclaimed, much shaken at the news.

Rosalind suddenly felt sorry for him in her usual generous way. To be sure, he had the most unfortunate manner, the most dreadful temper, but behind it all —

"I was in my garden when I heard the crash and her ladyship's scream," Mr Throckmorton went on, less aggressively, he too feeling some sympathy for the fellow, though he detested him. It was a shock for anyone to learn of such an accident to his sister. "I went out into the lane, and there she lay, unconscious in the middle of the road, the groom in a daze, with the phaeton quite wrecked and the chestnuts in panic. I think she must have hit the gatepost."

"What!" Sheldon roared. "She was driving *my* phaeton and *my* chestnuts? God, the little minx! She deserves to come to grief. This was a deliberate attempt on her behalf to get at me. As for the groom, I shall dismiss him on the spot for permitting such a thing." His face was so livid with rage he seemed like to go off in an apoplexy. "Are the cattle much knocked up?" he added with suppressed violence.

"Pray compose yourself, my lord," Simon said soothingly. "There is no harm to the beasts beyond fright. But the carriage, I fear — " He spread his hands in despair.

"Well, thank heaven nothing worse has befallen," Rosalind spoke up, speaking for the first time. "The horses might have been killed, and her ladyship into the bargain."

They all turned to look at her in surprise, the Rector with slightly raised brows, wondering who this odd female was the Marquis had brought with him. By her manner it was obvious she was not a servant, and it was unthinkable, judging by her appearance, that she was his lordship's latest flirt.

"Oh, pray allow me to present myself," she added forthrightly, catching the Rector's expression. "I am Rosalind Fenner-Smith, the Captain's niece. Lord Langton was at my uncle's house when the news of his sister's accident came, so

I came with him in case I could be of any assistance to him."

"That is very generous-spirited of you, ma'am," the Rector said warmly, "but there is really not the least need. Lady Letitia has every care."

"What, from your housekeeper?" Sheldon said scathingly. "She is used to the attention of a lady's maid. Come, Miss Smith, you had best come up with me after all. Throckmorton, if you will oblige by showing us the way."

Simon bit back the angry retort that rose to his lips, and without a word led the way up to his guest room. As he went, he was aware of the Marquis's critical gaze contemptuously taking in the shabby carpets, the faded wall-paper and scratched paintwork, the pile of clean linen hastily put out of sight on a chest on the landing at the top of the elegant curving Queen Anne staircase. But there was no shame in poverty, he told himself, and tried to ignore such uncomfortable feelings.

Sheldon stood looking down at his sister's still form, with her white face and bandaged head with the blood still seeping through. His habitual frown deepened into one of the utmost concern.

"The doctor was most insistent she not be moved, my lord," Mr Throckmorton's firm voice came from the discreet distance of the doorway.

"Yes, I understand," Sheldon returned gravely and rather unexpectedly. "It seems I am greatly indebted to you, Throckmorton. But for your timely action — "

"Yes, well, pray do not regard it," Mr Throckmorton said in some embarrassment. "I would have done the same for anybody."

"You will of course send the doctor's bill, any other expenses you incur in my sister's behalf, to me."

"Yes, my lord."

"Then I fear I can be of no use here. You have everything well in hand. I shall have some of my sister's clothes and personal belongings sent over as soon as possible."

"Pray, do not take it amiss, my lord, sir," Rosalind spoke up loudly, "if I nurse her ladyship. I have had a vast experience of such things. She must be carefully tended in such a case."

She was really an amazing woman, Sheldon thought. He said: "Thank you, I should be most grateful, ma'am. I'll know my sister is in good hands. I must own to it's being a trifle awkward at times, having no female relatives to hand. My other sisters and my aunts are scattered far and wide."

Rosalind glowed at such words from him. It was the nearest she had so far got to any civility from him. Had he told her he loved her, she could not have felt happier. Odd how she liked and disliked him all at the same time. She had never felt like that about a man before.

Leaving Rosalind with Lady Letitia, Lord Langton went down with the Rector to survey the damage to his phaeton.

"I will arrange to have it removed, and the horses returned to my stables," he commented grimly. "I hope this will teach my wilful sister a lesson."

My lord was in a foul temper indeed. He demanded that James be sent to him immediately. He ranted and raved at the poor man for a few minutes, then dismissed him on the spot, and would brook no argument. When the Rector tried to protest at such inhuman treatment, he told him to go to perdition in no uncertain terms.

"And while I am here, Throckmorton," Sheldon said, still in a fury, "there is that other matter to be settled between us, or rather, three matters, to be precise: repairs to the church, starting a Sunday School, and diverting the river across your meadow. Have you come to any decision as yet?"

"My mind is quite unchanged, my lord," Simon replied coldly and firmly. There was no dealing with such a callous man. "On no account shall I let you put the village at risk. My meadow remains as it is."

"Damn you for an addle-pated nincompoop, sir," my lord cried in vexation. "If that is your last word, may your church fall down before I give a penny to it, and as for your Sunday School, I'll see you in hell before I permit you to start one in my premises."

In great fury, he strode away to get his horse.

Mr Throckmorton sadly shook his head.

* * *

Lord Langton, on returning home, was not best pleased to be informed that Mrs Montagu had been waiting for him in the library for quite an hour or more. He went straight up to her, demanding as he entered the room: "What the devil d'you want, Josephine, coming at such an infernally inconvenient time? As if I'd not enough to contend with at present."

"Indeed, I'm very sorry," Josephine said huffily. "I thought you might be pleased to see me after so long."

"Now pray don't get uppish, my dear," he returned more placatingly. "But you have kept away from me so long, why bother now?"

"I am sorry to have so inconvenienced you, Sheldon," she returned sarcastically, "but I have been confined within doors. I have been slightly unwell."

"In that case, I suppose you may be forgiven. What ailed you, pray?" His tone was suspicious.

"Oh, a trifling cold, the merest thing," she answered hurriedly, not looking at him.

"Thank heaven for that. For a moment I thought — But no matter. You are recovered now, I trust?"

"To be sure," Josephine said flatly. How could she tell this harsh, unfeeling man that she bore his child, and that she was frantic with worry against the day her husband must find out, knowing it could not possibly be *his*? Involuntarily she clasped her hand over her stomach, realized what she was doing, quickly stopped it, and remarked with brittle brightness: "Roger is gone to Norwich. The day is ours."

"Oh, so that is why you are come, is it?" His tone was still sarcastic. "I thought there must be some reason. I was very ill received last time I called at Roselands."

"So that is why you have not been to enquire after me. Oh dear, Roger is acting so very strange of late. I quite begin to think the worm has turned at last."

"I'm quite sure he has."

"Do you then not want me any more, Sheldon?" she demanded bluntly.

He looked at her properly then. She was really very beautiful, very voluptuous, and he was damned if he'd take his marching orders from the likes of Roger Montagu.

"The devil! Of course I still want you!" he said thickly, suddenly pulling her roughly to him and pressing his mouth on hers while his hands wandered over her person.

"Roger will not be back till dusk," she murmured, running her fingers sensuously through his hair.

"We'll make the most of it, sweetheart," he responded, and carried her away to bed.

★ ★ ★

Simon Throckmorton heaved a sigh of relief as soon as Lord Langton was safely off his premises. Such a man was not to be tolerated. He then went to James and, having duly sympathised with him at such unjust treatment, offered to take him on for the time being as assistant odd-job man until he could find another post. The groom's gratitude was immense.

Mr Throckmorton, feeling that at least he had tried to do his Christian duty towards poor James, went indoors to discover how the invalid did. To him she was all sweetness and delight, and her only fault could be an excess of high spirits. Just the thought of her lying upstairs in the guest room filled his lonely Rectory with life and light.

Simon was brought down to earth with a bump by the sight of Miss Fenner-Smith descending the stairs, and saying loudly and prosaically: "Lady Letitia is beginning to sweat. I think she has a slight fever, but nothing to be alarmed about. I dare say she will come round in due course."

"Indeed, I trust so," Mr Throckmorton said fervently.

"Well, she is comfortable for the time being. I shall have to go to Long Croft and tell Mamma what I am about. She is quite used to me going off on these starts, but she likes to know where I am or she does worry so."

"Naturally, ma'am. But will you not first take refreshment with me? I was about to ask Mrs Craske to make some tea. So much more pleasant to drink in company than alone, don't you think?"

Rosalind agreed readily enough. She liked this well-meaning young man, who with his big nose, pale face, and pale sandy hair was halfway to being as ugly as herself. She willingly followed him into his best parlour, which even so was rather shabby and scantily furnished, and sat down the opposite side of the empty fireplace to him. It was rather chilly, but stoically she braced herself against it. Doubtless the poor young man could not afford a fire in his best parlour except on special occasions. She noticed he was looking very worried.

"You look quite out of countenance, sir," she said tactlessly. "Is anything wrong, pray?"

"No, that is, to be honest, Miss Fenner-Smith, yes, there is a great deal wrong."

"Oh dear!" she commented sympathetically. "Can I assist in any way?"

"The thing is, Lord Langton bothers

me vastly. For a start, he has dismissed his head groom without any notice, wages, or references merely for letting Lady Letitia drive out like she did. I have done what I can for the poor fellow, but that is beside the point. Langton is a heartless brute."

"Oh dear!" Rosalind said for the second time, adding generously: "I dare say he did it in the heat of the moment. One often says things one doesn't mean when one is angry."

"I dare say, ma'am, but Langton meant it all right. I believe it is not the first time he has done this kind of thing. But it is not only that. There is the matter of the church repairs, and the Sunday School, and my meadow. But of course, you know nothing of these things."

"Pray tell me, sir," she said eagerly. "There is often much to be gained by a fresh opinion on a subject, is there not?"

So, over a sober cup of tea, the Rev. Mr Throckmorton told his odd companion of his problems. He was glad to unburden himself to such a sympathetic but sensible listener. At the end of it, she set down her cup and saucer, and said decisively:

"Well, it is an excessively good thing I came to New Lyng, I declare. It is high time that odious Lord Langton was put in his place. I can see there is some plain speaking to be done with him. *I* am not afraid of him, and he is quite powerless to hurt me. But what is really needed is some action. *I* shall start the Sunday School, even if I have to hold it at Long Croft, and we will start a fund in aid of the church roof."

"I doubt we'd raise much in this parish," Mr Throckmorton said, hardly able to keep pace with this very decided young lady. "It is not large, and the people are not well-off, on the whole."

"There must be a few other large houses besides Lyng House."

"Well, there is Roselands, where Mr Montagu lives."

"Will not he help?"

"I am not sure. It is a little delicate, you see. Mrs Montagu is — ahem — she has a most irregular relationship with Lord Langton. You understand?"

"Oh dear, that dreadful man again!" Rosalind exclaimed in vexation. "How tiresome he is, to be sure! But I dare say that may be got over. The thing is, we must make it so that Lord Langton cannot hold a knife to our throats. What on earth does he want an ornamental lake for, in any event?"

"As to that, ma'am, I fear I cannot say. But I see what you are driving at. Only tell me, pray, why you should concern yourself so with the matters of this parish?"

"Oh, I am always sticking my nose in other people's business! Mamma says it is my greatest failing."

"It is an admirable quality when put to helping others."

"Well, I shall have to think on your problems. Now I must go and see Mamma and then get back to my patient

When she had gone, Mr Throckmorton felt as if a great burden had been lifted from his shoulders. He no longer had to fight Lord Langton alone.

Miss Fenner-Smith, sitting beside Lady Letitia's sick-bed, pondered the revelations made known to her by the Rector. The first thing she must do, she decided, was have a heart to heart talk with the Marquis, find out precisely what he was up to, why he was stirring up so much trouble in the village, and tell him straight that in no way would he be allowed to succeed. No doubt he would be back shortly to see how his sister did, and that was when she would tackle him.

All day Rosalind waited in expectation of Lord Langton's returning to the Rectory, and all day he did not come. Her vexation with him grew. Why did he not come? What was keeping him? Was he so selfish he did not care that his sister lay unconscious in a strange house?

Towards evening, Lady Letitia regained consciousness. Immediately Rosalind sent for the doctor again. He came at once, examined her ladyship, changed the dressing on her head, declared she was not near so bad as he had at first thought, gave her a sleeping draught, and took his leave, with a promise to return in the morning to see how the patient went on.

With Letty sleeping peacefully, and

darkness now completely fallen, Mr Throckmorton became insistent that Rosalind go home to rest, assuring her that he and Mrs Craske could cope now. While she hesitated, wondering why the Marquis had still not come back, he himself finally arrived. She heard his abrupt, rather imperious tones in the hall below ordering the house-keeper to take him up to Lady Letitia at once. He seemed not to have waited for Mrs Craske. His swift step was to be heard on the stairs, before he unceremoniously strode into the room.

"Oh, so there you are at last, my lord," Rosalind said at once, getting up to face him. "I had quite given you up for today. It is too bad in you. Whyever did you not come before, or at least send word to find out how your sister did? Don't you care about her?"

Mr Throckmorton was quite shocked at such outspokenness, though he secretly admired her for it. The Marquis himself looked rather taken aback. His habitual frown deepened slightly

"Of course I care, Miss Smith," he snapped back at her. "But I have been — " He hesitated only slightly before producing: "Somewhat detained."

"Indeed, my lord?" Mr Throckmorton stated with raised brows.

"Surely nothing is more important to you than your own sister's health and well-being?" Miss Fenner-Smith shot at him accusingly.

Why did this ugly, outspoken creature have to keep ripping him up so? Sheldon thought in annoyance. Did she imagine she was his confounded conscience? She certainly acted like it. And yet, thinking of his day of pleasure with Josephine, not to mention the young chambermaid he had been favouring with his attentions now for several weeks past, he had to admit in all honesty that temporarily Letty had slipped his memory, though it had not been intentionally. But annoyed as he was, he had no desire to upset Miss Fenner-Smith. For one thing she was right, for another she was the Captain's niece, and for another, incredible as it might seen, he liked her.

So he said in an apologetic, conciliatory tone quite alien to him: "I must confess myself at fault, ma'am. I stand corrected.

I have been grossly neglectful of my poor sister. Tell me, how does she?"

It would serve him right, Rosalind thought, if she had to tell him that his sister was worse, but she had the tenderest heart, despite her blunt manner, and looking hard at Lord Langton, she saw that there was deep anxiety in his dark eyes. Altogether, she decided, he seemed a trifle ill-at-ease, a trifle tense, the small scar on his left cheek more marked than previously. She wondered where he had got it.

She said quite gently: "See for yourself, sir. She is sleeping peacefully. She regained consciousness a while ago, and the doctor came again, and pronounced her not near so bad as he had first imagined. So you may be more easy now."

"Thank heaven!" he exclaimed fervently. "I am so greatly indebted to you, Miss Smith, and to you, too, Throckmorton. One does not expect to encounter such kindness in comparative strangers."

"Does one not?" Rosalind countered in real surprise. "That is a sad comment on the people you encounter, my lord."

The Marquis looked at her hard.

"You are the oddest creature, Miss Smith," he commented. "I should like to know you better."

"Well, I dare say you will eat your own words and be sick of the sight of me before long," she retorted briskly, to hide her own embarrassment at this unexpected compliment from this man who was beginning to disturb her so much.

Well, well, Simon Throckmorton thought, even he could not suppose the Marquis was making up to someone like Miss Fenner-Smith with a view to forming an improper relationship with her. That was inconceivable. The fellow seemed really quite moved. So had he misjudged him at all? Did the monster have some heart, after all? Was he really such a stranger to kindness? Did that account for his permanent ill temper?

Suddenly Mr Throckmorton felt very young, very inexperienced, and rather ashamed of himself. Oh dear, why did such an awkward man have to number among his flock? He could deal with an honest-to-goodness downright criminal far more easily.

"I was about to escort Miss Fenner-Smith home, my lord," he said aloud. "It is time she got some rest. My housekeeper and I can cope here for the present."

"Since you have both been at so much trouble on my account," Sheldon returned, his voice and manner still much softened, "it is I who must escort Miss Smith home. I am sorry, Throckmorton, I should have sent someone down from Lyng House to care for my sister. So remiss of me. My poor sister had died and I had not given her a thought. Whatever can you have thought of me? I must make amends to her tomorrow."

His listeners were so surprised at this little self-defamatory speech that they were both bereft of words for a moment, till Rosalind, pulling herself together, said in her habitual brisk manner: "Well, no harm has been done, so no use crying over spilt milk, eh? If you will kindly escort me home, my lord, I shall be most grateful. I shall return first thing in the morning. Thank you, sir," to the Rector, "for your hospitality. Good-night."

She extended her hand to the bemused Mr Throckmorton and shook his heartily, then, gathering up her cloak, she marched purposefully out of the room, giving Sheldon no choice but to follow.

"I'm afraid your only choice of conveyance is my horse again or Shanks's pony," Sheldon said, as they went out into the cold night air.

"I should prefer to walk, thank you. There is not the urgency there was before, and it is a bright starlit night. If you do not mind, that is."

"No, I never mind a little exercise. It is prodigious good for me, I am persuaded. Besides, it is not far, really."

She fell into step beside him, easily matching her pace to his long, athletic strides.

"It is not exercise I want, my lord," she told him. "It is the opportunity to talk to you."

"Did you have to go to such lengths to gain your end?" he asked with faint sarcasm.

"Yes, I did, my lord," she answered candidly, "since I want to talk to you alone. I think you will not quite like

148

what I have to say."

"I see," he said, his tone grim. "Are you going to lecture me further on my neglect of my sister, or has our precious Rector been talking to you? In either case, I must confess to being greatly disappointed in you, Miss Smith. I had thought better of you."

"I am sorry to disappoint you, though you have not precisely got the right of it. What I really have to say, sir, is that on no account will I permit you to put the well-being of the villagers here at risk merely to satisfy your own selfish whim. Furthermore, it is not the least use your threatening or trying to bribe Mr Throckmorton, because *I* mean to start his Sunday School for him irrespective of what *you* may say or do. And I design setting up a fund to repair the church roof, so we shall not be in need of your money for it, thank you."

Sheldon was flabbergasted. "Miss Smith," he said, struggling to keep his temper in check, "I have no desire to fall out with you, for I believe you to be a good-hearted, sensible sort of young woman, but you will kindly keep out of what is none of your business."

"Well, then," she retorted, "I have now made it my business, so you had best heed what I say."

"You would be much better employed looking to your widowed mother, ma'am," he flared at her. "For someone who has so recently suffered such a bereavement, you show remarkable lack of concern or proper feeling."

"*Proper* feeling, as you call it, my lord, is all a sham. Of course I mourn my father, but I scarce knew him, for he was always away at sea. I merely do not wear my heart on my sleeve. How then should I mourn too deeply for a man so little known to me, and make a great show of my grief, so that people point the finger at me in sympathy, when I could be much more usefully employed caring for the living who really need my help?"

"And what makes you think anyone in New Lyng needs your help, pray?" he demanded. "I suppose young Throckmorton told you I am about to drown them all in their beds? Do you always believe such tittle-tattle without first discovering for yourself the truth of the matter?"

"Do you then deny that you plan to divert the River Lyng?"

"No, I do not deny it, ma'am. But my purpose, much as you may discount it, is not to endanger the lives or property of the villagers, or even to disrupt their water supply, but to enhance the beauty of my park. I love beauty, Miss Smith, and I see nothing wrong in wishing to create it in this ugly world. Did you know that Lyng House is renowned for its beauty and good taste? It is in all the guide books. The number of visitors I get there when I have open days is quite astonishing at times. So the enjoyment is not for myself alone, you see. Though why the deuce I am endeavouring to justify myself to you I cannot conceive. To hell with you, Miss Smith, I don't give a damn what you say. You are as bad as all the rest of them."

"So you will not give up your scheme, my lord?" Rosalind said flatly, feeling an odd sense of hurt.

"Damn you, no, I will not," he cried violently, goaded beyond endurance.

"You will regret it, sir, have no fear of that."

"Then be it on my own head," he snapped back at her. "Now, have you quite finished threatening and insulting me, ma'am?"

"Not quite, though I meant no insult to you, believe me. I dare say you do not mean to be so tiresome."

"Tiresome?" he repeated, with one of his sudden loud hoots of laughter that so confused her. "Good God, you make me sound like a naughty schoolboy. I'd have you know, Miss Smith, I am a peer of the realm renowned for my scholarship in the ancient world and my knowledge and good taste in the arts in the modern one."

"I respect you for it, my lord, but all the scholarship and art in the world will not fill empty stomachs, make better ill health, or mend broken hearts."

"And pray what do you know of broken hearts, Miss Smith?" he cried, caught on the raw.

"Not my own, I confess, but other people's. Forgive me, sir, but it would seem that you, cocooned in your safe world of wealth and art and beauty, have no knowledge of anything beyond your own impressive park gates."

"I dare say I have as much knowledge as you, ma'am," he retorted, "of the suffering in this poor sad wicked dreadful world we live in. Perhaps I have not done so much about it as you."

"That is hardly to your credit, though I am glad you are honest enough to admit it. But it is greatly to your shame, since you are in a position to do much. Permit me to observe that you abuse your position, my lord."

"That is a matter of opinion. I pay my staff higher wages than anyone else in the county, I would say." Again, he wondered why he felt the need to justify himself to this preposterous horse-faced interfering female.

"Yes, and turn them off at a moment's notice without a reference the minute they displease you," she threw back at him with warmth. "Dare you deny that sir?"

"No, I do not deny it. It has ever been my practice, but you misjudge my motives, ma'am. It is not out of any

153

ill will or misanthropy I act thus, but merely in order to discourage idleness and corruption. A man or woman will be at pains not to lose something worth having if they know they will not get it elsewhere. I have no saucy kitchenmaids or lazy stablelads at Lyng House. They are all far too afraid of losing their positions and of not being able to get others."

"It strikes me as a heartless practice."

"Practical, merely."

"No relationship built up on fear can be good."

"That again is a matter of opinion. In general I have found it to be exceeding effective."

"As it was with James, your head groom?"

"Ah, so now we come to the crux of the matter, do we? You think me heartless and unjust in dismissing my head groom?"

"Yes, I do. At the very least you could have given him time to find *some*where to go, instead of threatening to throw him out if he was not gone by nightfall."

"I lost my temper, I fear," Sheldon

said, again feeling the need to justify himself. Confound the woman! "It has ever been my worst failing."

"Then at your age it is high time you learnt to control it, my lord," she said bluntly.

"My age has nothing whatsoever to do with the matter. Besides, I doubt you know it, in any event."

"You are being petty, now, sir."

"And you, ma'am, are being vastly insulting."

There was a short angry silence, during which they marched on side by side in the starlight. Eventually Rosalind ventured more quietly, but still pursuing her original theme: "Do you not care for human dignity? You turned that poor man out like a dog out of a kennel. Where do you suppose he has gone to?"

"That is quite his own affair," he said, still angrily. "He is no longer my concern."

"Impossible, unfeeling man!" Rosalind exclaimed in sheer vexation. "Do but consider. How would you go on if you were suddenly evicted from your home? Where would you go?"

"Since the likelihood is hardly possible, Miss Smith, I should be wasting my time in such idle supposition. Now pray be so good as to let the subject drop. I am tiring of this conversation. I wish you luck with your Sunday School venture, since it in no way involves me, and I am mighty glad to hear that at last someone is doing something about the church roof. It is high time it was attended to."

"I had hoped to appeal to your better nature, my lord," Rosalind said bitterly, "but I see now you have none. I am wasting my breath."

"There, Miss Smith, you are far out."

"Then you will take James back and promise to give up your scheme for an ornamental lake?" she cried eagerly.

"No, ma'am, I will not," he replied uncompromisingly.

"Then I will bid you goodnight, sir," she said with asperity. "You need escort me no farther."

Before he had a chance to say anything more, she strode off alone into the darkness.

Sheldon shrugged, and turned to retrace his footsteps. He was sorry to have fallen out with her, but her manner of addressing him and her ready assumption that he was at fault had put his back up. If she had approached him differently, less accusingly, he would have told her what he had told no one else, that he had no intention of causing harm to the villagers or anyone else either, that he had instructed a surveyor to find out what the real effect of diverting the River Lyng would be, and the best way to go about it without threatening anyone's property or water supply. There had been far too many wild rumours flying about concerning his proposals, and he meant to put paid to them once and for all. But so long as people expected the worst of him, it gave him great satisfaction to live up to their expectations of him. Nevertheless, he was sorry to have fallen out with Miss Fenner-Smith. He had looked for more understanding in her.

6

RIDING back alone to Lyng House, Sheldon felt oddly at variance with himself. For one thing, he had felt Miss Fenner-Smith to be stimulating company, and the way she had suddenly walked out on him had upset rather than angered him. He could hardly understand it. She was not even pretty, and in the usual way even mere prettiness did not attract him. So why now did he wish she was still beside him, when she had done nothing but find fault with him and abuse him? He even began to wonder if he had not been over hasty in turning off James. He was not used to questioning his own decisions, and it made him feel decidedly uncomfortable altogether, particularly over the matter of his thoughtless neglect of Letty. What in the world would Miss Smith have said if she had known what he had really been about: in bed with another man's wife, not to mention the chambermaid? He had no doubt she would have given him a thorough dressing-down, far stronger than any sermon delivered him by the Rev. Mr Throckmorton. The odd thing was, she struck him where it most hurt: on his conscience, but his was a perverse nature that would never admit to guilt, even when he knew himself in the wrong.

Well, he thought, as soon as he had had this survey done, and got the building of the lake under way, he would take Letty to London for a while. After all, she was old enough now, eighteen come July, and the change might do her good. It would also get her away from Mr Throckmorton's influence. As for himself, well, much as he loved Lyng House and his native county, he was getting tired of the quiet country life, he felt more restless and discontented than he had done for a long time. Perhaps, too, he wanted to get away from Josephine. If, as he half suspected, she was breeding again, he wanted to be well out of the way when the storm broke. He'd have no country squire's wife knocking on his door trying to serve a bastardy order on him. As for Polly the chambermaid, even the charms of a servant girl began to pall after a while, particularly when her belly began to swell. He would have to turn her off as soon as it became too obvious. She had served her purpose, and he did not want any child of his constantly thrown up in his face. He wanted fresh women, the companionship of men who shared his passion for the arts, and to hell with Miss Fenner-Smith and her preaching.

He sighed, feeling heavy hearted all at once. He did *not* want to send Miss Smith to perdition. He liked her too well, as he did her uncle the Captain. But she did not like him. So it always was. Few people really liked him, beyond those who appreciated his artistic knowledge and talent, his learning and scholarship of the ancient world. On more than one occasion he had been called to account for his association with other men's wives, thus the scar on his cheek, but he could honestly say he had never touched a woman who had not gone to bed with him willingly, which was more than could be said of some men he knew. But life was unjust and capricious, and he was no fool to believe it could be otherwise.

How different it might have been if only Amelia had not jilted him, he thought morosely. For all she had hurt him and humiliated him, in his heart of hearts he still cherished her, and were she to come back tomorrow — What would he do? She would be years older, for one thing, and in any event it was all idle speculation and a waste of time. He would continue to console himself with the likes of Josephine Montagu, amuse himself with the likes of Polly the chambermaid, and at his death Lyng House and all his titles and possessions would go to one of his cousins whom he scarce knew. It was a bleak prospect in some ways, but better than risking a second hurt.

Whatever happened, he would remove Letty to Lyng House the moment she was well enough, tomorrow if need be, then he would be beholden to neither that impudent young upstart Throckmorton or to Miss Rosalind Fenner-Smith.

But a wise man never makes plans for the morrow, he thought dourly next morning when he awoke with a throbbing head, aching limbs, and a throat so sore he could hardly speak, and, to crown all, a high temperature. Advised by his valet to get the doctor, he swore violently at that long-suffering gentleman's gentleman, told him to mind his own business, and vowed he would do no such thing. It was only a trifling cold, and he would get up presently as soon as he felt more the thing. All he wanted at the moment was a very large brandy and to be left in peace to sleep.

So Sheldon lay in bed feeling decidedly ill and very sorry for himself, and wishing that Letty was home. It was better having someone to quarrel with than having no one at all. As the day wore on, he felt worse instead of better. Hot rum and lemon with honey relieved the soreness in his throat for a while, but not for long, and blackcurrant cordial was hardly more successful. All he managed to eat was a little chicken broth. He did, however, rouse himself sufficiently to issue curt instructions for a servant to go over to the Rectory to find out how Lady Letitia did.

The next day he was so much worse, being very feverish, that he finally gave in to his man's pleas to call in the doctor, who duly pronounced him to have the influenza, gave him some foul-tasting medicine, and ordered him to keep to his bed and not have visitors.

For nearly a week Lord Langton lay in bed, hardly knowing what was going on about him and caring even less. Then, on the first day that he was allowed up, or even felt like doing so, he had a succession of visitors, who between them jerked him back into a sense of reality.

The first was Josephine, who swept in on him unannounced before he was scarce out of bed. He was half in and half out of his dressing-gown, his feet bare, his dark hair tousled, his face rather drawn and pale after his illness.

"Good heaven! Josephine! Must you come bursting in on me like that without even knocking?" he exclaimed in annoyance.

"Since when have we ever stood upon ceremony with each other, particularly in a bedchamber?" she retorted with a short laugh. "I thought you would be pleased to see me, Sheldon."

"Devil take it, I *am* pleased to see you. God knows I am heartily sick of chamber-pots and medicine and chicken broth, with no one to talk to but that fool of a man of mine."

"Well, how are you feeling now, my dear?" she asked with forced brightness, unfastening her redingote and seating herself in the fireside chair.

"I am no use to you yet if that is what you mean, Josephine," he said crudely.

"Tut, Sheldon," she returned with a brittle laugh, "a good thing my husband cannot hear you."

"Cutting up rough still, is he? Why must he start behaving like a vulgar country squire about it after all this time?"

"Because he *is* a vulgar country squire," she affirmed, a hard light in her fine blue eyes.

"So what have you done with him at present? How have you managed to escape from his clutches this time?" His tone was sarcastic, though his voice was a little weary.

"He is gone to visit old Sir Matthew

164

Drayton near Lynn. I feigned a headache."

"Prodigiously ingenious of you, my dear." His tone was even more sarcastic. "I applaud you. God, I feel weak!" he ended, as he took a step across the room.

"I could leave him," Josephine stated baldly. "Roger, I mean."

"What?" Sheldon roared incredulously. "Why the devil should you want to do such a crack-brained thing as that, pray?"

"To be with you, of course," Josephine answered bluntly, though, now the moment to tell him the truth had come, she was inwardly quaking. This was not a very promising start, to be sure. Perhaps she had picked the wrong moment.

"We have always gone on perfectly all right as we are," Sheldon retorted, though with a sense of foreboding. He had an idea he knew what was coming. "I have no wish for anything to change."

"If I don't leave, I dare say Roger will throw me out soon," she said in the same matter-of-fact tone.

"He may dislike our relationship excessively, and rant and rave about it, but his bark is worse than his bite. He'll not dare throw you out for fear of the scandal."

"He will when he knows I carry your child."

"I see," Sheldon said grimly, but not yet conceding defeat. "And what's to stop him thinking it's his? He is your husband, after all, and it's the natural conclusion to come to."

"It would be if we had lain together in recent months. But he never comes near me these days."

"*Confound* it, woman!" Sheldon cried violently. "Why the deuce didn't you tell me before?"

"Would that have made so much difference?"

"Every difference. I'd have left you alone. Are you sure of this?"

"Absolutely certain. So what shall you do about it, Sheldon?"

"Nothing," he replied at once. "You should not have deceived me."

"*I*? Deceived *you*?" she cried angrily. "Fie, sir, rather have you been taking advantage of me. I'll tell you one thing, Sheldon Howard, if you abandon me now I'll scream it from the housetops what you've done to me."

"And d'you think I give a damn for that, ma'am?" he shouted back furiously. "Why the hell should I care what you do? You are nothing to me. What do you take me for? A charitable institution for misbegotten brats of careless high-born ladies?"

"I'll *tell* you what you are, Sheldon Howard," she shrilled at him hysterically. "You're a damned cold-hearted, self-centred, odious, selfish, heartless *pig*!" She ended, pleading desperately: "*Please*, Sheldon, don't abandon me, I beg of you."

Sheldon recoiled as if from a physical blow, seeing not Josephine's face but Amelia's, hearing not Josephine's voice but Amelia's, spitting just such vituperations at him as Josephine was now doing. So had she walked out on him those dozen years ago. A fierce pain burnt in his heart, scorching his very being. Could it be Amelia had been right about him? Had he been deceiving himself all these years? Was he really such a heartless brute?

"Sheldon, did you hear me?" Josephine screeched at him.

"For God's sake don't shriek at me like that," he snapped, his temper rising again. "I detest above all things, hysterical women. I did hear what you said. But do you suppose you will make me help you by calling me names and abusing me in that vulgar fashion, for I assure you you will not?"

"I beg your pardon," she said more quietly, trying to swallow her anger.

"Why did you have to spring this on me when I feel so damned weak? I am scarce up from my sick-bed."

"There you go again," she cried fiercely. "All you think of is yourself."

"The same might be said of you," he retorted, but less heatedly.

He looked at her hard. He was only one of a long succession of men in her life, he knew, as she was of women in his. He did not love her at all, but they had had some pleasurable times together. She was not Polly the chambermaid, to be dismissed as an inconvenience that he had no further use for. Suddenly with his confused thoughts of Amelia there came disturbing memories of Rosalind Fenner-Smith, who pulled him up at almost every turn. Her verdict on him at present would be scathing indeed, he felt sure.

"Go home, Josephine, if you please," he said wearily. "Pray do not plague me at present with such problems. I have no notion what may be done as yet, but rest assured I shall not abandon you. Something may be worked out, of that I am persuaded."

She gazed at him uncertainly.

"I am not quite heartless, my dear," he said, going to her and patting her hand reassuringly. "Only pray do not say anything to your husband as yet. Will you promise me that?"

"Of course," she replied at once, an edge to her voice. She was suspicious of his sudden turnabout, giving in to her demands. She had expected such an ugly scene, instead of which, he was being almost kind. This was not the Sheldon Howard she knew. What had happened to him? Was it the low state of his health, or what? In any event, she did not wholly trust him. She had been foolish ever to get embroiled with such a man. She got up to go, adding as she did so: "I trust you feel more the thing soon."

"Thank you. I trust so too."

"Good-bye, Sheldon," she almost snapped at him, and without even kissing him she marched from the room for all the world as if she scarce knew him.

Sheldon had little time for retrospection. He hardly had time to recover from his first visitor before his man came to announce that Captain Fenner-Smith was below stairs desiring audience with him.

"Good God, am I to be continually pestered?" he exclaimed irritably, though he was much astonished at such a visitor.

"He begs to see your lordship most urgently," the man informed him.

"Very well, but not until I'm dressed. I'm damned if I'll receive him in my dressing-gown and slippers. It puts one at such a disadvantage. Be good enough to attend to your duties, Smithers, and assist me to shave and dress. I feel devilish."

Some time later, Lord Langton insisted on making his way down to the library to receive his guest. Captain Fenner-Smith, awaiting him there, noted with some surprise that his friend did not walk with his usual brisk stride, and at once planted his tall, powerfully-built athletic frame in a chair close to the fire. He was rather pale and drawn, and the habitual frown that marred his otherwise comely features was rather one of worried preoccupation than the usual discontent.

"I am sorry to incommode you, Langton," the Captain said at once. "I perceive you are still far from well."

"I am tolerably well recovered, thank you. But it is always rather a blow to one who is never ill to be confined to a sick-room. It shatters one's belief in one's ability to shift for oneself."

"Alas! That has been only too true in my case," the Captain said sadly. "This curst leg of mine has been the curse of my existence. However, one learns to live with one's disabilities in due course."

"My greatest disability, I fear, is my own damned temperament. I have never been of a happy disposition." His tone was rueful. "And you are one of the few people I'd admit that to, Smith. Now I regret to say I seem to have got myself in a tight corner with a woman. I am beset by problems at present. No matter. What did you want with me that, forgive me, you leave your lair to come to me?" He had been so preoccupied with his own affairs that he had not noticed how white and drawn his visitor looked, the lines on his lean face deeply etched. It shocked him slightly. He ended in some concern: "Surely you have not walked all the way here?"

"How else should I get here, pray? I would not take my sister-in-law's carriage."

"My dear fellow, you must be quite done in. Let me offer you something. What will you have?"

"Brandy, of your kindness," the Captain replied thankfully.

Sheldon got up and went to a side table on which stood decanters and glasses. He poured out two generous measures, gave one to the Captain, then returned to his chair with the other.

"Thank you," Crazy Mick murmured.

"Well?" Lord Langton demanded in his abrupt way. "What is amiss, pray?

How can I assist you?"

Not at all put off by his lordship's tone of voice, the Captain drank some brandy before answering.

"I have had a letter from my wife," he said at length.

"Good God!" Sheldon exclaimed, quite taken aback. "After all this time? What the devil does she want?"

"She had heard of my brother's death, and sent me her condolences."

"I suppose she thinks there is something to be gained from you now you are your father's sole heir," Sheldon commented dourly.

"Oh dear, think you so, my friend?" the Captain said worriedly. "I must confess I never thought of that. Do you always see the worst in everyone?"

"Only as everyone does in me. But why else should your wife bother to write to you without she had some ulterior motive in mind?"

"Perhaps you are right. It was something of a blow to hear from her out of the blue like that. I had to talk to someone about it. I own myself greatly disturbed by it."

"Does your sister-in-law have knowledge of this?"

"Indeed, no. I could not talk to her. But you, Langton, who have suffered at a woman's hands yourself, you understand, I feel."

"Forgive my curiosity, Smith, but did she say anything else at all?"

"She gave me her direction, informed me she was well, and regretted her impetuous folly of twelve years ago."

"As I thought, she is trying to make up to you, by the sound of it."

"Langton, you must help me," the Captain said in great agitation, gulping down the rest of his brandy. "What if she comes back to me? What shall I do?"

"A week ago you seemed to want her back," Sheldon reminded him bluntly, getting up to refill their glasses. "Only you can know what you want, though the question has not arisen as yet. For myself I should have nothing more to do with her."

"Not even if the young woman who once jilted you came back to you?"

Sheldon paused, his hand on the brandy decanter suddenly very still.

"There you have me, Smith. I have asked myself the same question a hundred times over. I simply do not know."

"Did you love her very much?"

"Prodigiously so. I have never quite got over the blow of her leaving me like she did. But I was very young then, and very green. I hardly think my own case has anything to say to yours. Nevertheless, I have every sympathy for you, and will do anything I can to help you, of course I will." He handed the Captain his brandy, and sat down again. "But I'd not fret unduly as yet if I were you. Your wife may have no intention of returning to you. So be at ease while you may, my friend."

"Yes, I will try. Thank you, Langton."

"Now, pray do stop awhile and bear me company, then I will have the carriage take you home. I would drive you myself if I felt more the thing."

"I would not dream of permitting you to do so, my friend. But certainly I will stay awhile. I have missed your visits to me sorely this past week. I had not realized you was not well till your servant informed me of it, though I had wondered at your staying away so long. I had thought perhaps you wished to avoid my niece. She never told me you were laid low."

"I doubt she knows. No doubt she believes me completely heartless and therefore indifferent to my sister's plight that I do not call at the Rectory in person to enquire after the chit. I have not enlightened her. She has no very high opinion of me, I fear, and no very great liking for me, either."

"She has an unfortunate forthrightness of manner, but is otherwise a very good sort of girl, I believe. I am persuaded you mistake. In any event, do not mind what she says."

"On the contrary, I mind her very much," Sheldon said with a faint smile. "She talks remarkable sense, and is right in most everything she says about me, except about my feelings for my sister. I find her most stimulating, even if she does make me lose my temper, but that is not hard to do."

They sat in companionable, pleasurable solitude, drinking steadily and rather heavily, the Captain filling the room with his pipe smoke. When the latter eventually rose to go he was a trifle unsteady on his feet, but very happy, and even the hard-headed Lord Langton felt excessively mellow.

After his friend's departure, he sat on in his library, still drinking steadily, and staring into the leaping fire, trying to sort out his rather muddled thoughts on Amelia, Josephine, and Rosalind. Polly the chambermaid did not count for anything. He was a little put out, therefore, when his third visitor, and one of the objects of his thoughts, marched unannounced into the room.

"I could not wait for your servant to decide whether to admit me or not," Rosalind Fenner-Smith said in her strident, forthright way. Her penetrating glance took in at a sweep the empty brandy decanters, and the faint touch of colour in Lord Langton's cheeks, which she mistakenly supposed to be from the drink, but which in actual fact was from the heat of the fire. "So that is the way of it, is it, my lord?" she went on knowingly. "I perceive you have consumed a prodigious quantity of brandy. It is a wonder you are not stoned out of your mind."

"I have not drunk all that amount myself, ma'am," Sheldon immediately rushed to his own defence. For once her bad manners in walking in on him unannounced eluded his reproof. He was hardly aware of the fact that she had done so. In truth, he found himself exceedingly pleased to see her again after so long. "Your uncle has not been gone from here above half an hour at most."

"If you have got my uncle drunk, sir," she retorted tartly, "you will have my mother to answer to."

"It takes little assistance from me to get him so," his lordship muttered.

"For shame, sir, you are in no very good condition yourself. I heartily hope you may be horridly sick. 'Twould serve you right."

"Brandy never makes me sick. I have a strong head."

"Then more shame to you for encouraging others who have not."

"I might have guessed you only came to rip me up as usual, Miss Smith. I had hoped you might have come to enquire how I did. So much for my hopes. More fool I."

Drink at least had the beneficial effect of softening his temper, Rosalind thought philosophically. She said aloud rather sharply: "As to that, I care not a rap what may come of you, since you see fit to forget all about your poor sister."

"I have not forgotten about her at all," he said indignantly.

"You have ignored her completely all week, apart from that one impersonal message you sent days ago. She could have died for all the thought you have given her."

"How can you know my thoughts, ma'am? They would surprise you, I've no doubt. In any event, I knew my sister was well enough in your capable hands."

She might be rather lumpy and shapeless, he reflected, gazing at her a little hazily, but she had beautiful large breasts and child-bearing hips. If one only kept one's eyes shut, she would no doubt be very good in bed, only supposing one could ever get her there, which seemed rather unlikely.

"Oh, how odious you are!" she exclaimed crossly, quite unaware of the desire she was beginning to rouse in him. Brandy always made him rather lecherous. "Such selfish unconcern goes beyond belief."

"If you must know, ma'am," he said, rather more sharply, annoyed by her assumptions about him, "I have felt too ill even to enquire after her, even to care."

"Oh!" she said, pulled up short by this revelation. So she had misjudged him. It had never entered her head that he might be ill. Poor man! And she had said such dreadful things to him. "I am excessively sorry. I had no notion," she continued more gently. "But why did you not acquaint me with the fact?"

"Why did you not bother to enquire?" he countered.

"I thought to see just how long you would stay without bothering to come near your sister," she confessed unashamedly, "to prove to myself how selfish and heartless you really are."

"And I sent no more messages out of sheer perverseness, to see how long you would think so ill of me." He gave one of his loud shouts of laughter, and put down his empty glass. He had no need of brandy now he had Rosalind Fenner-Smith. The annoying thing was, he was dying to relieve himself, yet had no wish to go and do so in case his companion left while he was gone. So he resolutely crossed his legs in an effort to ease the discomfort in his lower parts.

Nothing, it seemed, missed her piercing gaze.

"If you wish to go to Jericho, sir," she said, her voice as strident and unabashed as ever, "you may do so. I shall not be put about at all. It is a perfectly natural function, after all, and we all have to do it. I shall not run away while you are gone."

For one of the very few times in his life, the Marquis of Langton blushed scarlet in embarrassment. Was there nothing this astonishing creature would not say?

"Of course," he said abruptly, and got up to leave the room.

While he was gone, Rosalind very deliberately removed the empty decanters and glasses from near his chair, and placed them on an occasional table near the door. Then, first removing her cloak, she sat herself down to await Lord Langton's return.

He was not long. When he came back, his colour was still rather high, and for a moment he avoided her gaze.

"I trust you are feeling much better now, my lord," she said brightly, "both from your visit to Jericho and from your illness."

"Much, thank you," he said shortly.

"Oh dear, I fear I have offended you, or at least your sense of propriety, or perhaps your pride or your dignity," she stated anxiously. "Pray forgive me. I meant not to. It is just my way always to be blunt."

He sat down again, feeling strangely unnerved in her presence.

"You do not have to apologize, Miss Smith. It really does not signify in the least."

"Oh, but it does. I have put you to the blush, and that I did not mean to do. I beg your pardon."

"Never mind."

His temper, she thought, was still very

much mellowed by the brandy.

He changed the subject. "Tell me, how does my sister now?"

"She is greatly recovered, I am pleased to say. Indeed, she has been up and about these four days past."

"What, and you did not let me know, when you knew I wanted her home as soon as possible?" he cried, with some anger.

"That is quite your own fault for not bothering about her," Rosalind retorted without sympathy. "The thing is, Lady Letitia stated quite emphatically that she did not want to return home. She says you are more like a jailer than a brother and guardian."

"I see," he said in an expressionless voice.

She glanced up at him sharply, and was surprised to catch the hurt look on his face. So he did care, after all. He was not quite a heartless brute. The knowledge filled her with a sudden glow of happiness, and she smiled warmly at him.

"Never mind, I dare say she did not mean the half of it, sir," she said, trying to soften the blow.

"Oh, but I am persuaded she did," he retorted quickly. "We have never hit it off well together. I try my best for her, but it is never right. Only the morning of her accident we had an argument and she threw the sugar bowl at me. See here, I have the proof of it." He held out his hand to her, where his knuckles still bore scabs from where the sugar bowl had grazed him. "And that is the least of some of the things she has done to me from time to time. I am a mere helpless male and cannot cope with her."

"Oh dear!" she murmured sympathetically, taking advantage of an opportunity to touch him again by laying gentle fingers on his hand. A tiny thrill of pure delight trickled through her. "And I was quite taken in by her and believed every word she said. What a complete hand she is, and what a ninny you must think me."

"Not at all, Miss Smith," he said, smiling faintly at her. "I am only glad you do not think me quite such a monster now. So what would you have me do with my sister, pray?"

"In due course, let her marry Mr Throckmorton and settle at the Rectory," she replied simply. "They are head-over-ears in love with each other."

"What?" he cried, leaping up in sudden incredulity and fury.

"I know it is very sudden, and they have only known each other for a short space, but — "

"But nothing. I never heard anything so outrageous. My sister and that — that prosing young nincompoop of a parson. My God, girl, what the devil do you take me for? I will accept no less than a Viscount for my sister, for one thing, and for another, to encourage such a damned whippersnapper to make up to Letty is quite intolerable, the grossest insult to myself. That fellow is opposed to me in everything I am and have and do, and would set out to turn my sister's silly head merely to spite me."

"No, you mistake, my lord. Mr Throckmorton is the most well-meaning young man, and if he is opposed to you in any way — Well, I dare say it is all a gross misunderstanding. He only seeks to protect his flock against any exploitation by you."

"Poppycock! He is a snake in the grass. And my sister would imagine herself in love with him merely to spite me, too. She must come home instanter."

"You are acting very unwisely, my lord. I have seen Lady Letitia and Mr Throckmorton together — "

"When I want your advice, Miss Smith, I'll ask for it, I thank you," he interrupted cuttingly. "I'll send a carriage to fetch her right away."

"You will only make her more contrary and difficult to handle. Let her stay a while longer — "

"I'm damned if I will. Apart from anything, it would not be proper. Which puts me in mind of something. Do you mean to say you have left my sister with that fellow?

"No, I don't, my lord. My mother is with her ladyship at present."

"Why the deuce must your confounded family take it upon themselves to nursemaid mine? I like not to be beholden to anyone for anything."

"I dare say you need nursemaiding,

that is why," she shot at him. "You do not seem very able of coping with anything properly yourself."

"How dare you — " he began angrily.

"No doubt because I was born on All Fools' Day. That makes me out a fool."

"That is no answer. I was born on Christmas Day, but that does not make me out a saviour of mankind."

"No, that is too true," she said with much feeling, and laughed suddenly and rather loudly.

Sheldon stared at her in amazement for a moment, then he too began to laugh.

"By God, what a combination!" he exclaimed. "All Fools' Day and Christmas Day. Our parents ill-timed our conceptions, did they not?"

"Oh, yes, indeed, sir! What a shock for any woman to have you for her Christmas box."

"And how inappropriate your birth day was, for you are no fool, Miss Smith, far from it, call me what you will."

They stopped laughing as suddenly as they had started, and were left staring at each other with a new awareness. He was really excessively good-looking when he was not scowling, Rosalind thought. Perhaps he needed to laugh more often.

"I must be going," she said rather self-consciously.

To her surprise he took her hand and raised it to his lips.

"Thank you for raising my spirits, Miss Smith," he said quite gently. "Also for bearing with me, and for caring for my sister. I should like for you and your mother to wait upon my sister and myself as soon as is convenient to you. Your uncle also. I have the greatest regard for your uncle. I know you are still in full mourning for your father, but 'twill be quite an informal visit. Do you sing or play upon the pianoforte?"

"I sing like a cow in pain, and the only thing I play is cards, and that scarce ever, for I hold it to be a vanity, a waste of time. My only accomplishment is upon the globes, and that only from following my father's progress around the world when I was a child. But I should like of all things to come, if only to prove I bear you no ill will for anything at all."

"That is vastly noble of you, to be

sure, a worthy sentiment, even if I do not follow it myself. As you must have deduced, I am a great one for bearing grudges."

By his tone it was difficult to tell if he was being serious or not, so she merely muttered something unintelligible, gathered up her cloak, and made for the door.

"Mark my words, you will be sorry you were so high-handed with your sister," was her parting shot. "Good-day to you, my lord."

7

AFTER the departure of his last visitor, Sheldon felt shattered, tired, worried, and something else he could not quite define, something that concerned Rosalind Fenner-Smith. But first and foremost there was his sister to get home, so duly he issued strict orders to the servants thus accorded the task that on no account must they come back without her ladyship, or they would suffer instant dismissal. While he awaited their return, he sat by the library fire, a couple of handsome red-setters at his feet, pondering the problem of Josephine. She would have to be got rid of, that much at least was plain to him. He wanted no part of any child of his not born of love. But how best to accomplish this, without creating too much scandal, or too much cost to himself, or too much hurt to anyone, was quite another matter. Certainly he did not want to be saddled with Josephine for the rest of his life. At least, thank heaven, she was married, so there was no danger of his having to marry her. Married women and servants were always safest game, when the inevitable happened, as it had several times with him. He could never really be brought to account. Only that once when he had been called out. The scar on his cheek bore permanent witness to the fact.

Thinking along these lines, he remembered Polly. It was high time she was sent packing. Even he could see that she was now several months gone in pregnancy. Accordingly, he sought her out, and gave her instant dismissal. She screamed and cried and pleaded and made a dreadful scene, all to no avail. He in turn begged her to be reasonable, but finally lost his temper, called her a designing slut, and told her to get out at once.

In the worst of bad tempers, with his head beginning to ache furiously, Sheldon returned to the library, only to be stopped in the Stone Hall by the enactment of another high tragedy in the form of his sister being forcibly dragged

191

into the room by a stout footman and a sobbing abigail.

"Cease that caterwauling at once, Letitia," he ordered angrily, beginning to wish he had never got up that day, "and try and conduct yourself with a little more propriety."

"I don't *want* to come back," Letty stormed. "I hate you, Sheldon Howard. Why couldn't you let me stay where I was happy?"

"Leave her to me," Sheldon commanded the two servants, and grabbing hold of his furious sister dragged her into the library and closed the door firmly after him. At once she bit his hand and kicked his shin, so that he exclaimed in pain.

"You little vixen!" he cried, sucking his injured hand. "Don't you dare move, or I shall put you over my knee and spank you — *hard*!"

There was an ominous silence. He turned to look at her, and was taken aback to see tears in her eyes. Now that her fury had spent itself, she looked very pale and woebegone.

"Letty, pray be reasonable," he begged more quietly. "You have to come home, you know that. Where else are you to go? You could not remain at the Rectory indefinitely. It would not be proper."

"Not nearly so improper as when you go to Roselands," she retorted. "At least I was *wanted* at the Rectory. You did not even come to see me. I think you wanted me dead. I wish I *was*."

"Don't be nonsensical. Of course I do not want anything of the sort. I couldn't come to see you. I was in bed with the influenza. I have only got up today for the first time."

"I wish you might have had the smallpox at the very least. But I mean to marry Mr Throckmorton, and you won't stop me. I shall run away if I have to."

"For heaven's sake, Letty, what on earth are you talking about? Apart from anything else, you scarce know Throckmorton."

"I have known him quite long enough to know that he is everything you are not. He is kind and generous and patient and unselfish and virtuous and — and *poor*! And I love him, so there!"

She choked on a defiant sob, the tears poured down her cheeks, and she groped frantically for her handkerchief."

Sheldon stared at her in helpless dismay.

"Don't you care for me at all, Letty?" he asked. "I have tried to be a good brother to you. But can't you see how impossible 'twould be for you to marry Throckmorton. He is, as you say, poor, and could not keep you in the style you are accustomed to. Apart from that, you would soon get bored as the wife of a country parson. Furthermore, he is far below you in birth and breeding."

"As if I give a fig for that."

"He is totally unacceptable to me as a husband for my sister and ward," Sheldon said uncompromisingly. "Besides, have you no loyalty to me when you know full well that Throckmorton is my sworn enemy? If I cannot look to my own sister to back me up, who can I look to?"

"I owe you no loyalty. I would not back you up in any of your selfish, evil schemes if I was your wife, even, which thank heaven I am not. You are quite odiously horrid and completely heartless, and I wish this was France, then you'd have been guillotined long ago."

Lord Langton had turned rather pale. He regarded his young sister steadily.

"Is that what you really think of me, Letty?" he asked quietly. "Or are you merely quoting Throckmorton, or speaking in the heat of the moment?"

"It is what I really think of you," she threw back at him without hesitation.

"Well, I am sorry for it. I had not thought I had been so unkind to you."

"Not to me so much, but to others."

"Is there nothing I can do to make you change your opinion of me?"

"Nothing."

"Nothing at all?"

"Well, you could give up your scheme for an ornamental lake."

"That I will not do. I have set my heart on it."

"Or take poor James back into your service."

"That I cannot do. 'Twould undermine my authority with the other servants."

"There, you see," she cried accusingly. "You will not budge an inch on any point. You are a lost case indeed."

"I would have repaired the church at my own expense, only your precious

Rector would have none of it."

"What? How can you say so? You made him a wholly unacceptable offer. You should have done it without any conditions attached."

"I wish to God I had, but I will not go back on my word."

"You will do nothing except what benefits yourself," she said contemptuously. "Mr Throckmorton says — "

"I will not have that fellow's name mentioned again in this house," he raged suddenly, quite losing his temper. "If ever I catch you going there again, or trying to contact him in any way, I'll lock you up and feed you on bread and water. So help me I mean it. I'll see that damned upstart in hell first before I'll let him make up to a sister of mine again."

"Well, we'll see about that," she yelled at him, and fled from the room.

★ ★ ★

Simon Throckmorton sat in his study, trying to write his sermon for Sunday, something he was finding it increasingly difficult to concentrate on, for his mind would keep wandering off to Lady Letitia Howard. With him she had proved to be everything he had hoped for, a warm, generous, eager spirit, certainly lively and rather strong-willed, but none of the things her brother had made her out to be. It seemed it was only he who brought out the worst in her. Given something worthwhile to channel her energies into, she was little short of an angel, Mr Throckmorton thought. Without her, not only his Rectory but his whole life seemed dull and empty. There was only one thing for it, he would have to brave Lord Langton's anger, and beg for her hand in marriage. Yet he could well imagine what the Marquis's reply to that would be. He'd probably throw him out of the house for his presumption. And indeed, compared to Lady Letitia herself, he had nothing to offer her, only this shabby Rectory and his stipend, not even any noble relations. His grandfather had been a humble clerk in Exeter, whereas the Howards were connected with some of the highest in the land, and held vast estates and fortunes and titles. Oh dear, why was life fraught with so many difficulties? Why, of all people, did he have to go and fall in love with the sister and ward of a man like Langton, a man who seemed to be his sworn enemy? However was the problem to be got over, for he would never give up hope of making Lady Letitia his wife? But it was a problem that would have to solve itself in due course. In any event, it was early days yet.

For the next few days, Mr Throckmorton found life strangely empty. He missed Lady Letitia's lively presence very much, and found it hard to concentrate on his sermon, his parishioners, or anything else. All the while he found himself thinking of her ladyship and wondering how he could contrive to see her again. Then something happened which quite took his mind off everything else.

He had gone to bed early as usual, about ten o'clock, and promptly fallen asleep. About two hours later, he was awakened by the sound of his dogs barking frantically in the yard below. He turned over, buried his head in the pillows, and tried to ignore the sound.

But he could not. It was too persistent. Obviously something was wrong.

Heavy limbed and half asleep, Mr Throckmorton stumbled out of bed, groping for his bedside candle. By the time he had found it and lit it, and pulled on his shirt and breeches, his manservant Henry was knocking urgently on his door.

"Sir," the man cried, as the Rector opened the door, "there be men in the meadow."

"Great heaven!" Mr Throckmorton exclaimed in alarm. "What manner of men, pray?"

"'Tis hard to rightly say, sir. But men with lanterns, staves, and shovels. And dogs, sir."

"Dogs, eh? Then 'twould seem they are up to no good. I had best come at once."

"Best be careful, sir. I don't like the sound of they dogs. Mighty fierce sounding, they be."

"There's only one person to whom my meadow has any value," Simon remarked throughtfully. "Only one who would dare come under cover of darkness with staves and dogs to keep off intruders."

"Milord Langton, you mean, sir?"

"Precisely, Henry. I fear it seems as if he has decided to carry out his wicked plans illegally, against all advice and better judgement and proper feeling. What on earth does one do with such a fellow, I ask? I do not want a pitched battle on my hands, with possible resulting bloodshed or worse. Yet at all costs he has got to be stopped. There is nothing for it. I shall have to try and reason with him, or appeal to his better nature, only I am persuaded he has none."

"Might not be him, sir," Henry ventured.

"Well, we had better find out," Mr Throckmorton said resolutely, putting on his coat. "Keep the dogs in, Henry, at all costs, but bring some stout staves."

"How about the garden fork, sir?"

"No, not that. I do not want to carry more than the minimum of defensive weapons, or the matter could get out of hand. As yet we do not know what we are up against."

Armed with only a stout stick each,

with the dogs safely shut up in the yard, Mr Throckmorton and Henry, the former carrying a lantern, trod carefully through the darkened Rectory garden, through the gate and into the meadow beyond. Across the far side were shadowy figures of men and dogs to be seen moving about by the dim flickering lights of lanterns. It certainly did not look as if there was any digging being done. At once, the dogs set up an excited, fierce barking.

"Who's there?" Simon called loudly, though his voice shook a little, and he began to break out in a cold sweat as the forms of two large dogs broke away from the group and came bounding towards him, growling and barking by turn.

"Heel!" ordered a familiar cultured voice sharply, and at once the dogs obeyed. Mr Throckmorton breathed a sigh of relief, thankful beyond everything that Lord Langton was at least not an out-and-out savage to set his dogs on an innocent man — at least, not yet!

"My lord, you are trespassing on my land," the Rector called out boldly.

"Throckmorton, the devil!" came the angry exclamation.

"I repeat, sir, you are trespassing," Mr Throckmorton reiterated firmly. He could just make out the Marquis's tall, powerful figure striding across the meadow towards him.

"You are an interfering little busybody, sir. Go home," Lord Langton told the Rector, towering menacingly above him. "That way no one will get hurt, least of all yourself."

"You are trespassing, my lord," Mr Throckmorton said doggedly.

"Damn you, don't keep repeating yourself, sir," the Marquis snapped irritably. "I heard you the first time. I know full well I am trespassing, but since you would not co-operate with me, I have had to take matters into my own hands."

"I have little opinion of you, my lord," Simon stated, at his most pompous, but mainly because he was quaking in his shoes at having to stand up to this inhuman tyrant, "but I had not believed even you would stoop to carrying out your evil schemes in utter defiance of my wishes by going about it stealthily, by night, armed with dogs and staves and guns, too, for all I know, against all comers. For shame, sir!"

"Go to the devil, you prosing young upstart," my lord cried furiously. "Think what you will, do what you will, but you won't stop me. And I advise you to get your facts right first, or you will soon be made to look a fool in any court of law."

"The facts speak plain enough for themselves, my lord," Mr Throckmorton retorted. "And I care not what kind of a fool I am made to look so long as I succeed in putting a stop to your wickedness."

"My God, what arrant nonsense you do talk," the Marquis scoffed, with a harsh laugh. "Now go back to your bed, before I *do* set my dogs on you. So far I have restrained them, for I have no wish for anyone to be hurt, even you, but I do not make threats lightly, as you will learn to your cost if you do not heed my advice."

"I will not go meekly back to my bed at your bidding while so much is at stake, my lord. Henry," he turned to his servant who stood respectfully at a distance, "come with me. We will put a stop to this once and for all. Pray stand aside, my lord."

"Cease this tomfoolery at once!" the Marquis snapped, not moving an inch.

"If you do not stand aside of your own free will, my lord," Simon said quietly but dangerously, "I shall be forced to remove you."

"Try, sir," his lordship challenged.

The ensuing battle was to be talked about in the village of New Lyng for weeks to come, how the local Rector came to blows with the Lord of the Manor when the latter refused to get off the former's land. It was a short and sharp struggle, in which the Reverend gentleman struck one blow at my lord, and was instantly floored by a regular facer planted on him by my lord's powerful left hand (my lord being left-handed, a childhood disability that no amount of threats, punishment, or scolding had been able to correct). The Rector's servant Henry had rushed to his master's defence, wildly brandishing a stout stave, with which he had proceeded to clout the Lord of the

Manor across the head. This action had immediately brought his lordship's men to their master's aid, followed by his two handsome red-setters, who between them succeeded in frightening poor Henry out of his wits and sending him fleeing to the safety of the Rectory. By this time the rest of the Rectory servants had appeared on the scene, rather too late to help their master other than to carry him back to his bed to have his injury tended to. My lord the Most Noble Marquis was more fortunate, being made of far sterner stuff, and quickly regaining consciousness, had got to his feet, brushed himself down, sworn violently when he had felt the lump on his head, and directed his men to get on with their work, setting the dogs this time to keep guard. The Lord of the Manor had won the first round against the Rector, the tyrant against the people's champion, and the villagers were consequently angry, alarmed, and dismayed.

But the Marquis was quite undeterred, and next night his men, this time armed with pistols with instructions to shoot if need be, were again at work in the

Rectory meadow, while the Rector lay, angry and helpless, nursing his injuries. Two days later, Lord Langton was to be seen, fully restored to health after his influenza and his bump on the head, taking his usual daily exercise, riding hard across the parkland.

Sheldon rode for several miles, exhilarating in the exercise, glad to be back in the saddle again after nearly two weeks. The bitter cold wind blowing off the North Sea cleared the cobwebs away, making him feel much refreshed and lighter in spirit. The affair with the Rector had put him in an exceeding ill temper, added to which Letty had not spoken a word to him since that first outburst on her enforced return, the new parlourmaid who had roused his desire had rejected his advances, still the problem of Josephine was unsolved, and he had not seen Rosalind Fenner-Smith since her visit to Lyng House. His illness had taken a greater toll of his strength than he had bargained for, a crack on the head had not helped at all. Today was the first day he had felt more like his normal self.

When his mount began to tire, he

turned her about and headed back for home. On the way, he made a point of going by the church to take another look at its sad state of repair. Viewed with his expert's eye, it looked worse than ever he had at first supposed. He doubted it would stand against a really strong gale. It would certainly not wait till Miss Fenner-Smith had raised enough in her fund for the purpose of putting necessary repairs in hand. The graveyard, too, displeased his fastidious eye, being somewhat neglected and overgrown.

Trying to lift the depression that threatened to settle on him again, he then went to view his extensive greenhouses, which always gave him great pleasure. He spent more than an hour there with his chief nurseryman, discussing various points of rearing and propagation. It was while he was thus employed that his head gardener came to him with shattering news.

"Milord, thank heaven I've found you," the man cried breathlessly. "The most dreadful thing. I don't know who ever could have done such a thing. All broken down, ruined."

"What the deuce are you babbling about, man?" Sheldon demanded impatiently.

"The walled gardens, milord. All trampled down, everything quite flattened. All the plants. It must have been done in the night. I only discovered it while your lordship was out riding."

"Good lord!" Sheldon exclaimed incredulously, light beginning to dawn. "Are you telling me someone has deliberately broken down the plants in the gardens?"

"Not only plants, milord, shrubs as well, and young trees. Such destruction you never did see."

"My God!" Sheldon said, too stunned even to be angry.

"I've been in the orchards all morning, and only went into the walled garden not long since," the head gardener informed him. "I could scarce believe my eyes. There it all was, deliberate as you please."

"You had best show me."

"It weren't my fault, milord."

"No, I attach no blame whatsoever to you."

The man breathed a sigh of relief. At least he would not get turned off as James and Polly had done, for something not his fault.

Lord Langton followed his head gardener to the walled gardens, and there stood stock still in disbelief and dismay, staring at the destruction of his prized plants and shrubs and young trees. It was just as if a herd of elephants had rampaged over them.

"My God!" Sheldon said for the second time, much shaken.

"Who on earth could have done it, milord?"

"I wish to heaven I knew. But I can make a few guesses. I have many enemies about here."

"What shall I do about it, milord?"

"Clear everything. Burn the lot. Dig it all in," Sheldon exclaimed, suddenly angry, and strode furiously away.

His was a vengeful nature. He would not rest until he had sought out and punished the culprits. Meanwhile, he issued strict orders for the dogs to be set loose, and for certain of the outside male servants to keep a lookout for any intruders. Despite all this, the destruction of the garden had come as a severe blow to him. He'd had no idea he had roused so much animosity in anyone, especially since he was at such pains to make sure he harmed no one by his schemes. Of course, there was James the dismissed head groom, and the dismissed pregnant Polly, but they alone could not have perpetrated such a revenge on him. He would pursue every possibility in tracking down those responsible for such wanton damage.

His sister did not help matters by breaking her silence to say to him: "Well, I hope you are well served, brother. Now you will see just how odious everyone thinks you."

He gave her a hurt look, but did not answer, unable to dispute the truth of her words.

"Have you nothing to say then?" she demanded.

"What is there to say?" he countered. "The damage has been done, and, according to you, I have got my just deserts."

"Do you not have anything to say in your own defence?"

"Nothing at all. I do not consider I

have done anything wrong. If I am not guilty, why therefore should I defend myself? I have been misjudged merely. That is quite another matter."

"Oh, such odious self-opinionated pomposity!" Letty cried in disgust. "You say you have done nothing wrong when everyone knows you set upon the Rector, and set your dogs upon him, and knocked him down, just because he told you you were trespassing on his meadow, which you *were* doing, trying to start diverting the river across it without his permission by working stealthily by night."

"Think what you will," Sheldon snapped harshly. "It is a gross distortion of the truth. Even you cannot think me such a fool as to believe I could divert a whole river in a couple of nights without being found out."

Letty was taken aback. She gaped at her brother.

"*Were* you not diverting the river?" she asked.

"It is scarce any of your business."

"Oh, you are impossible!" she exclaimed angrily.

Shortly after this little exchange, Sheldon's

vexation was greatly increased by the unexpected arrival of Rosalind Fenner-Smith. This time he received her in the grandeur of the Stone Hall. At sight of her all his desire for her flared up again, much to his disconcertment, though he was genuinely pleased to see her. Her first words, however, soon made him realize that she did not feel the same about him. In fact, she was decidedly out of temper with him.

"For shame, Lord Langton," she greeted him in her strident tones. "What on earth do you suppose you are at, carrying on some nefarious business in the Rectory meadow by night and knocking down the Rector? As for your heartless dismissal of Polly — "

"So you have come to lecture me, have you, Miss Smith?" he said, to her intense surprise not at all angrily. "I was foolish enough to hope you might have come to see how I did?"

"What?" she cried in astonishment.

"Oh, pray do not look so surprised, Miss Smith. You have such a generous heart, such a well-meaning soul, I am persuaded, that I had thought perhaps your goodwill might extend even to me. Had you forgot I was ill in bed for a week, and did you know that your precious Rector's manservant clouted me over the head with a stout stave and temporarily knocked me out? Have you not a little sympathy for me, for no one else has, except perhaps your uncle, but he has problems enough of his own?"

She looked at him in even greater astonishment, not sure if he was funning or not. He was regarding her with an odd expression she could not define but which disturbed her greatly, an expression that no other gentleman had ever bestowed on her. He really had quite a nice face, she thought, when he was not in a temper or an ill humour, which to be sure was unfortunately not often.

To cover her confusion she said tartly: "I am sure a lecture will do you far more good than any sympathy, my lord. You have behaved abominably."

"I am sorry you think so. I had thought I had acted for the best."

"You are the only one to think so. However, I suppose it is something that you believe you acted for the best and did not deliberately set out to harm anyone."

"I only do that when I feel justified in being revenged on someone."

"For shame, sir," she reproved him. "However, in all charity I am compelled to enquire after your health and well-being, since you seem so cast down and sorry for yourself. I trust you are much mended since last I saw you?"

"Much, I thank you, but no thanks to you. You did not see fit to come and minister to me as you did my sister."

"That would hardly have been seemly, my lord."

"As if you'd give a fig for that if you really wanted to do something," he retorted. "Be honest, Miss Smith, you did not want to nurse me."

"In your case it was hardly necessary, my lord. You have a vast army of servants at your beck and call, and more than enough money to pay for everything you want."

"True enough. But that is scarce the same thing as having someone care for you because they hold you in some esteem. Do you know, Miss Smith, were

I to drop dead tomorrow I doubt there is anyone would really mourn me."

"Dear me, you have got a fit of the dismals, sir," Rosalind exclaimed cheerfully.

"So would you have if a person or persons unknown had just broken down all the plants in your garden, as I have just had."

"Good gracious, do not say so!"

"Indeed, I do, ma'am."

"Then I am vastly sorry for you. Two wrongs never did make a right, and I am sure even you do not deserve quite such unkind using, for my uncle tells me how much you care for your garden and greenhouses."

"Indeed I do, and I thank you for your sympathy. You know, Miss Smith," he went on reflectively, "you really should take more care of your person, have a little more dash and style in your dress, do your hair in a more fashionable way, perhaps even eat less to lose some of those unsightly lumps, for to be honest, I consider you have the most beautiful hair and complexion, and your eyes are rather fine."

He was regarding her in a very disturbing manner, half critical, half admiring. She was completely confused, blushing furiously, not knowing what to say, how to take him, whether to be angry or complimented or what.

"Poor Miss Smith. I have put you to the blush, I fear," he said gently yet mockingly. "Well, now we are quits, for you put me to the blush last time we met, and that is something no woman has done before." His voice softened still more, the mockery now quite gone from it. "Pray do not be offended, ma'am. I mean no insult to you. I like you too well, even if you always make me lose my temper with you. Let me see how you look without your spectacles."

As he spoke he raised his hand and lightly lifted her spectacles off her nose. She trembled at his touch, and a shock like electricity ran through him. For a brief moment they stared into each other's eyes, a mutual desire and liking flaring up between them.

"On second thoughts, I think you had best keep them on, Miss Smith," Sheldon said, trying to speak lightly, though very much shaken. He had never felt quite like this about a woman before, not even Amelia.

"This really won't do at all, my lord," Rosalind said sternly, trying to pull herself together, and adjusting her spectacles. Right at that moment she would have liked nothing better than for Lord Langton to pull her into his arms and press his mouth on hers. It was rather a shattering experience for her, since in the usual way she never bothered about men except if they needed ministering to. Not counting, of course, various youthful fancies she had briefly entertained long ago but who had dashed her hopes by being completely indifferent to her, hardly surprisingly, she had come to think, seeing how ugly and shapeless she was. Now she could hardly belive that suddenly she should be attracted to this man, of all people. Even more astounding was the fact that he, who had good looks and shapeliness and elegance, apart from anything else, should seem to reciprocate her feelings. It was against all rhyme and reason, since they were opposed to each other at almost every turn. He stood for privilege, ruthlessness, tyranny and self-interest, everything she was against. Yet her feelings were so strong she was quite helpless to fight against them.

"You are quite right, ma'am," he agreed. "It won't do at all. I trust I am a gentleman, at least, if you will allow me no other good or agreeable qualities."

"No gentleman, sir," she said, finding convenient refuge in anger, "would have used poor Polly as you did."

"Good God, what business is that of yours?" he retorted, losing his temper at once. "What a damned busybody you are, to be sure. Is nothing and nobody free from your meddling?"

"With people like your lordship around, it is as well there is someone to meddle in an endeavour to counteract your evil cruelty and ruthlessness," she flung back at him. "How could you turn off a poor defenceless girl whom you yourself ruined?"

"Who said it was I?"

"Do you then deny it?"

"Not at all. Why should I? But the wench is a pert chit, and I'll warrant I'm not the first nor the last to have my way of her."

"*That* has nothing to say to it," Rosalind almost shouted at him in sheer vexation. "You have an answer for everything, have you not? Well, I design that you shan't forget her in a hurry. You will be constantly reminded of her, for I have persuaded my uncle to take her into his service."

"*What!*" Sheldon roared furiously. "How dare you, woman? You really are set on raising the dust, aren't you?"

"Not at all," she answered firmly, facing up to him squarely. "Merely to right a few wrongs. What's more, my lord, next Sunday we start the Sunday School in an outhouse at Long Croft. It is not precisely what I should have liked, but it will serve well enough for the time being, and Mr Throckmorton is prodigious pleased with it. And I have opened the fund for the church roof, and Mr Montagu of Roselands has given most generously. I explained to him that he must set a good example in the parish, being the most prominent resident after your lordship, but as your lordship

219

refused to donate to the fund — "

"My God, you are a snake in the grass, ma'am, aren't you?" Sheldon cried angrily.

"And I have promised your sister I will escort her to wait upon Mr Throckmorton to see how he goes on," Rosalind delivered her final thrust.

"That I will *not* allow," Lord Langton fumed.

"You can scarce stop me, my lord, short of locking your sister up."

"That I am quite capable of."

"That I can well believe," she shot back at him. "I think you are quite capable of anything. A man who can stoop to the level of knocking down the Rector to gain his own ends is beyond contempt. Going about your wicked business armed with staves and vicious dogs — "

"There you are far out, ma'am. My dogs are *not* vicious, and if my men were armed with staves it was purely for their own protection, not for attacking others. And my business in the Rectory meadow, to which I presume you allude, was not wicked. I was acting for the good of myself and the village, even of

Throckmorton himself, if he only had the sense to see it. But I am not answerable to you, and if you believe such gossip, then think what you will and go to the devil."

She looked at his angry, good-looking face, and had a sudden horrid, guilty suspicion that perhaps she had misjudged him, at least on one account.

"I dare say you think you are acting for the best," she said more kindly, "even if you are not. That makes you vastly more tolerable than if you were deliberately doing wrong."

He gave one of his sudden unnerving shouts of loud laughter.

"My God, Miss Smith, I do believe you mean it. That's rich, that is! No, pray do not look such daggers at me," he added quickly. "In all seriousness, I am mightily obliged to you. That is the greatest kindness anyone has shown me this age past. How greatly happy and honoured I should be if only you would champion *my* cause instead of Throckmorton's. But I can see that would be *too* much to ask."

She turned away to hide her blushes.

How silly, she thought, annoyed with herself. Just like some simpering, missish schoolgirl being paid her first compliment by a young gentleman. Only she wasn't a schoolgirl. Far from it. She would be eight-and-twenty come All Fools' Day, which was only days away. Which made it even more ridiculous. Surely she was not going to be so stupid as to fall in love with this overbearing, ill-tempered, selfish man? Unfortunately, it seemed only too possible.

"Pray, Miss Smith," he went on more gently, as she did not speak, "let us be done with quarrelling for the present. You have dealt me enough blows already, and scored one over me at every turn. Make it up to me by coming here tomorrow with your mother and uncle to sup with me. Pray do not deny me that one kindness."

She turned to him with a glowing smile that made her, at least to him, appear almost pretty.

"Thank you, my lord, I should be most honoured," she said. "I bear you no ill will at all, you see."

8

SHELDON was so delighted at the prospect of Rosalind and her family coming to visit him that he was in a good mood all the next day, much to the surprise of his household, who had never remembered him so good-tempered or benevolent for such a long period at a time. Letty was quite civil to him, and unbent sufficiently to be quite talkative to him about everyday subjects, though she carefully avoided the subject of the Rev. Mr Throckmorton, and even the new parlourmaid finally yielded to him and invited him into her bed. He even managed to forget about Josephine for a few hours.

About eight o'clock the family from Long Croft duly presented themselves at Lyng House, despite its being a wild wet night. The Marquis received them in the White Drawing Room, a chamber not as impressive as the Stone Hall, being furnished in a more modern manner, but very grand for all that, with delicately flowered white silk hangings on the walls, elegant white furniture upholstered in white printed silk, with an immense glass chandelier, and a full-length portrait over the white marble fireplace of the present Marquis's mother and himself as a small boy in petticoats at her side. Lord Langton himself was dressed informally but very elegantly in pale buff pantaloons so tight as to seem moulded to his powerful athletic form. His frock coat was of discreet dark blue superfine, the frilled cuffs of his shirt showing below the close-fitting sleeves a pure spotless white, as was his neckcloth. He sported a single fob only at his waist, and his dark hair was brushed in the most fashionable of dishevelled styles. Most remarkable of all, though, was the smile that brightened his usually scowling countenance.

"You look positively agreeable, my lord," Rosalind exclaimed in delighted surprise, as she gave him her hand.

"Oh, pray forgive my daughter, sir," Mrs Fenner-Smith said apologetically. "Her tongue does run away with her so at times. She means no offence."

"Don't worry, ma'am," Sheldon said politely. "I find your daughter wholly charming." As he spoke, he raised Rosalind's hand briefly to his lips, though he purposely avoided her eyes. He was astonished but gratified to note that she had pinned up her beautiful pale red hair, and wore pearl drops in her ears. The effect was to enhance her fine high cheek-bones, making her whole face look slimmer, and giving her dignity.

"You do not have to be gallant to me, my lord," she said in her loud way.

"I assure you I am not, Miss Smith," he returned with a smile. "I am speaking the plain truth."

"Oh!" she said flatly, wholly nonplussed, and blushed scarlet. She glanced up, saw the portrait over the fireplace, and said wildly, clutching at straws: "What a remarkably fine picture, sir."

"That is my mother, thirty years ago and more," he responded at once. "And that brat is myself, two years of age."

"Good gracious!" she exclaimed, much struck. "I had not thought someone like yourself could ever have been the age of innocence."

"I sometimes doubt it myself," he laughed. "But there you have the truth of it. I'm told my mother doted on me, as her only son amongst so many daughters. For seventeen years I have only remembered her death."

"Is that why you are usually so ill-natured and short-tempered?" she asked bluntly.

"I dare say," he returned with rare good-humour.

"You *are* in a prodigious good mood this evening," Rosalind could not refrain from remarking. "I cannot conceive of its being possible."

"It is *you* who have wrought this miraculous if temporary change in me," he told her.

"I? How could I? What have I done?"

"You have made me very happy, ma'am," he answered simply, and turned away abruptly to greet her mother before his feelings got the better of him and he said more than he meant to or more than was proper.

Mrs Fenner-Smith, who had been talking to Letty, now stepped forward and bobbed Lord Langton a little curtsy, which he acknowledged with the slightest of bows.

"I am honoured by your visit, ma'am," he said formally, but, nevertheless, meaning it.

"The honour is all ours, for sure, my lord," she returned. She was not quite sure yet what to make of this lordly aristocrat, and stood rather in awe of him. "But I am glad of the chance to have speech with you. My poor brother-in-law seems so disturbed of late, especially so since receiving another letter from his wife yesterday. He is like a cat on hot bricks, and can scarce sit still for two minutes together. Something has greatly overset him, and 'twould seem to be in some way connected with your lordship's self."

"Good God! Are you sure, ma'am?" Sheldon cried in astonishment. "What on earth can I have done to overset him?"

"I do not mean that, precisely. I do not think it is anything you have done, but — Oh dear, I do wish you would speak with him, try and draw him out. He is so dreadfully close. But he has the greatest regard for your sense and judgement."

"Has he, indeed? I confess I am all astonishment, ma'am. But I will see what I can do. I should hate to be the cause of any distress to him for I esteem him prodigiously. Surely he does not believe this current nonsensical gossip that I have surreptitiously been digging up the Rector's meadow to flood you all in your beds, does he? For if so, I can assure him I have more sense."

"I am relieved beyond everything to hear you say so, my lord, though I thought it must be so. There has been such talk in the village against you. Now I can set people's minds at rest."

"No, pray do not say anything at all, ma'am," Lord Langton, with a sudden return to his habitual manner, almost snapped at her. "It is nobody's business but my own, and I make such assurances only to you as my friend. But it was of your brother-in-law we were talking, I believe."

"Yes, of course, sir," Mrs Fenner-Smith said hastily, thinking what an awkward, disagreeable man he was, to be sure, and how easily and inadvertently one might provoke him. For all that, there was something about him she could not help liking, and at times she almost felt sorry for him, his seemed such an unyielding temperament, such an unhappy disposition.

For the first part of the evening Sheldon had no chance to talk in private with Captain Fenner-Smith. Letty, with very little persuading from the visitors, was prevailed upon to show off her skills on the new Broadwood pianoforte the Marquis had recently bought, accompanying herself in a pleasant, tuneful but rather childish soprano. When her ladyship happened to mention that her brother could sing much better than she could, it took much more persuading from the mother and daughter and uncle to get him to join in. With the greatest reluctance he finally agreed to do so, completely taking his little audience by surprise and admiration with the richness, melody, and superior quality of his voice. They were most enthusiastic, and afterwards clapped most vigorously, begging him for more. But he firmly declined, saying that he would far rather listen to Letty.

"What a dark horse you are, to be sure, sir," Rosalind took the opportunity to say to him as Lady Letitia struck up a lively song by the celebrated Mr Charles Dibden. "What other secret accomplishments have you got, pray?"

"None, I doubt, except perhaps a proficiency in Hebrew and Ancient Greek, and I have variously dabbled in architecture, archeology, and the designs of parks and gardens. When young I had a desire to follow in the steps of Capability Brown, only of course I did not, and Sir Humphrey Repton has done it instead."

"Then it is a pity you did not, for you have wasted your talents sadly, and have made a great nuisance of yourself into the bargain, whereas you could have been a useful member of society."

"I have ever preferred the pursuit of my own pleasure to anything else, and have been fortunate enough to be able to afford to follow it."

"Insufferable!" Rosalind burst out angrily. "How you can dare confess to such shameless selfishness — "

"At least I am honest about it," he defended himself, cutting her short. "I have never pretended to be other than I am. You cannot accuse me of humbug."

"I wasn't going to!" she exclaimed in vexation.

"Be quiet," he ordered. "You talk too much. You will put Letty off her piece."

At which Miss Fenner-Smith was so surprised that she shut up immediately.

Soon after this supper was served, not the homely informal gathering round the parlour fire it was at Long Croft, but a lavish repast served on silver platters by gold liveried footmen. It seemed, Rosalind thought, that the Most Noble Marquis of Langton would tolerate nothing mean or shabby about him, everything was in the first style and elegance, no expense was spared to gratify his own taste for beauty and perfection. Perhaps he was too much of an idealist, she reflected, perhaps then it followed he got hurt and disillusioned too easily. This notion made her look at him in a new light, and the dawning of a new understanding of him came to her.

After supper, cards were brought out, and a sober game of whist proceeded, the stakes being set very low, at least by Lord Langton's standards, in accordance with Miss Fenner-Smith's wishes, as, she declared roundly, she deplored excessive gambling, or excess of any sort.

Eventually, leaving Letty to entertain the two ladies, Sheldon took the Captain away to the sanctuary of the library where they could enjoy a glass of port together.

"My sister-in-law is very well in her way, a most good-hearted sort of woman," Crazy Mick said in confidence to his host, "but her being brought up a Methodist does tend to restrict a fellow somewhat."

"I know precisely what you mean," Sheldon returned sympathetically, "but I have been lucky enough never to suffer in that way. My female relatives are too far away, apart from Letty, and she gives me quite a different kind of hell. Mrs Fenner-Smith, though, I am sure, is only concerned for your well-being. She confesses to being worried about you. I do not wish to pry into your private affairs, my friend, but *is* anything troubling you? You have perhaps heard from your wife again?"

The Captain drained his glass and waited for it to be refilled before he replied.

"Indeed I have, sir. I have been wanting to tell you ever since I heard. She informs me she is coming into Norfolk to see me."

"Good God! After all this time! What can you suppose she is after?"

"She realizes I am now my father's heir, and, God willing, will one day be *Sir* Michael Fenner-Smith, which will make her a Lady. She is that kind of greedy, grasping woman, as I remember."

"Good Lord! I do not envy you, man."

"The thing is, she does not say when she will arrive. It could be tomorrow, it could be in a week or even a month's time. But that is not all. I feel I should tell you, Langton — "

At that moment there came the sound of an explosion, as if in the bowels of the earth, while at the same time the whole house seemed to shake, and shattering glass was to be heard from the direction of the East end of the building. The candles flickered and dipped, and some went out.

"My God, what on earth is it!" the Captain cried in alarm.

"The devil!" Sheldon exclaimed simultaneously.

"An earthquake, surely," the Captain said, a little more calmly. He had gone very white. "Or perhaps the French have invaded us."

Sheldon himself was rather shaken.

"I think not, my friend," he remarked, going to the window, pulling aside the curtain, and peering out into the darkness. "An explosion, rather."

"Do not say so! What kind of an explosion?"

"That, sir, I mean to find out," the Marquis said grimly, and letting the curtain fall back into place, strode purposefully from the room. The Captain hesitated only a moment, then hurried after him.

The house was already in uproar, with servants scurrying hither and thither in panic. The cause of the explosion was very soon apparent. Someone had deliberately sabotaged the pump-house in the small courtyard adjoining the East wall of the house, and flames were now issuing forth from that quarter. The menservants were immediately organized into a human chain bearing buckets of water from the pump in the stableyard, their efforts proving futile, however, till his lordship's private fire appliance was brought out from the coach-house and put into use. The fire, which turned out to be only a small one, was then quickly brought under control. But the damage to the pumping mechanism was serious indeed, and meant that all water for internal use at Lyng House would have to be carried over from the pump in the stable yard until effective repairs had been carried out. Some of the windows had been blown in in the lower floors, but otherwise the main block had suffered no damage.

Lord Langton was furious, and only courtesy to his guests prevented him from rushing straight out to try and find the culprits. Instead he strode back indoors to return to the White Drawing Room to make his apologies. He was soaked to the skin, his thin indoor shoes sodden, his hair dripping in loose curls about his face, which, together with his hands, were filthy with grime and smoke. To his surprise he found Captain Fenner-Smith limping along painfully at his side. He too was soaking wet and grimy.

"You must go directly and change your clothes, Langton, else you will catch your death, so soon after being ill," the Captain said firmly. "I will make your apologies to my sister-in-law and niece, and see them safely home. No need for you to trouble yourself. They will quite understand, in the circumstances, of course they will."

"But you are quite as dirty as myself," Sheldon said in great surprise, forgetting for a moment to be angry. "Do not say you have been out there — "

"I could not stand by and watch my friend's house burn down — though I admit that seemed hardly likely in the event — and not do anything about it, could I?"

"Could you not?" Sheldon returned, deeply touched. "To be sure most others could. I am excessively obliged to you, Smith. I trust you have done yourself no lasting harm by your noble action."

"But who could have perpetrated such an outrage, my friend?" the Captain queried. "It is quite monstrous, I declare."

"By God, it is!" Sheldon cried savagely, his anger returned. "As to who did it, sir, why, Throckmorton, Montagu, James my ex-head groom, the whole village for all I know. They all believe they have a grudge against me. But behind it must be someone who has the wit to acquire gunpowder. No peasant could do that alone."

"I suppose not. But you have certainly stirred up much malice against yourself, though surely no one would go so far as to — "

"Someone *did*, though, did they not, and By God I mean to find out who. I'll make such an example of them no one'll dare raise a finger against me again."

"That is quite your own affair, of course, Langton, but take a word of advice from an old sailor who has seen much of the darker side of life. Shipboard life is no bed of roses, and lashing is often the only answer to such wrongs as are committed, though my niece insists it is barbarous and only makes men more cruel. But one thing I learnt as Captain, my friend, and that is that a little kindness often goes a long way."

"Thank you," Lord Langton said curtly, barely containing his fury, "but I am quite able of handling my own affairs, and I am not the Captain of a ship. Pray excuse me, Smith, I am in foul rage, and have no wish to distress you. Goodnight. I will make my apologies to your family tomorrow."

He strode away, leaving the Captain sadly shaking his head.

Sheldon had hardly got out of sight and sound of one Fenner-Smith before he bumped into another: Rosalind, her face streaked with wet and filth, her hair flying out of its pins in long damp tangles, her black mourning dress soaked and clinging to her lumpy figure. He stared at her in astonishment.

"Miss Smith, what the devil have you been at? You are quite as infernally filthy as myself."

"Here's a pretty to-do!" she exclaimed, with a laugh. "We both look like a couple of chimney-sweeps."

"You have never been out there in all this rain, have you?" he cried angrily. "That was no place for a woman."

"Oh, fustian! Of course I was out there, helping carry buckets of water."

"Preposterous creature! What in the world am I to make of you? What prompted you to such foolhardy action, when you might have been sitting snugly in the White Drawing Room with your mother and my sister?"

"To be frank, my lord, I was so angry that someone should do such a thing to you. Your whole house could have been burnt down."

They stared at each other, she with the full realization that she did indeed love him, he with the knowledge of some emotion he could not quite define, for always there was Amelia and the wound in his heart that she had inflicted.

"I trust you thanked your servants properly for their efforts in your behalf," she said sternly, to hide her true feelings.

"Of course I did not," he retorted at once, nettled. "Why should I? They are paid for it, and well paid at that."

"It costs nothing to say thank you, my

lord," she told him tartly.

"As I have just been told by your uncle that a little kindness goes a long way," he shot back at her. "It seems that your family are full of sound maxims and good advice for me tonight, and I am not in need of either, I thank you. Go along, Miss Smith, your uncle is gone to look for you in the White Drawing Room to take you home. Go before you make me angry and fall out with you."

"*That* does not take much doing," she said bluntly.

"Goodnight, Miss Smith," he said firmly. "I am only sorry the evening had to end like this. Thank you for your efforts in my behalf."

"You do *not* have to thank *me*," she retorted, and hurried away.

Sheldon had little sleep that night. Taking fresh clothing with him and throwing a heavy cloak over his wet self, he strode through the soaking rose walk to the stable yard, not for the first time in his life wishing it was not so far away and separate from the house. There he washed himself down under the icy water of the pump, dressed in the comparative warmth of the sweet-smelling stables, put on the cloak once more, and sallied forth to inspect more closely the damage done to the pump-house. It had been put completely out of action. It was indeed a fair enough revenge on him if only he had really been out to endanger the village water supply. The infernal thing was, he had not. He had gone to great lengths to avoid any such possibility. Thank God no further damage had been done, or anyone hurt. But first the walled garden, now the pump-house, what next? Would whoever it was stop there? He could not take the risk of waiting to find out. The time had come for some decisive action. And he knew precisely what he would do for a start: close the park to all comers.

He lay awake for a long time listening to the wind howling about the house, the rain beating against the windows, and found himself wondering how the decaying fabric of the church would stand up the wildness of the night. He knew, as a native of Norfolk, what Throckmorton and Miss Fenner-Smith, as newcomers, did not: just how furiously the gales could blow across the county, uprooting giant trees, stripping roofs, hurling down chimney-pots, even, from time to time, church towers.

And tomorrow he must be up at the crack of dawn to ride into Norwich to make arrangements to have the pump-house repaired at once. He would trust no one else, not even his steward, with such an important task. People would jump at a word from him when they would not for a mere steward.

He was good as his intention, and was away to Norwich at daybreak. He made short shrift of his business, and was back in New Lyng by mid-afternoon. Before going home, he took the road round his park till he came to the Rectory. He had only one thing in mind, to find the devil who had sabotaged the pump-house, and the Rectory was as good a place to start his search as any.

He had not supposed he would get a very warm reception at the Rectory, but he had hardly bargained for practically having the door slammed in his face by a stony-faced housekeeper. However, he was quick to guess her intention, and thrust his booted foot in the door.

"How dare you shut the door in my face, woman," he fumed, "when I call in a perfectly civil manner? Stand aside if you do not wish me to remove you bodily out of the way."

"It's all right, Mrs Craske," the Rector's voice called down the hall. "Pray allow his lordship to enter. It is high time he and I discussed the matter between us."

"Very good, sir," the woman said reluctantly, and stood back to let the Marquis in.

In the hall the two men came face to face, the younger one sporting a badly bruised face and a half-closed right eye.

"Good God, did I do that?" Sheldon was moved to exclaim.

"You did, my lord," Simon answered grimly.

"Well, it is no more than you deserved. Though I am sorry for it. It is not right for gentlemen to *brawl* in such an ill-bred manner. And your manservant repaid me in full with that crack over the skull he gave me. I have a lump on my head still, and confoundedly sore it is, I can tell you,"

"I too am sorry for it, my lord, but I know you did not come for that."

"No, indeed. Have you heard what happened at Lyng House last night?"

"I have, sir. And if you can suppose I was responsible for such a monstrous piece of work — "

"I did not say so. I trust not, for your own sake. Only you can know that at present, though I mean to get at the truth of the matter in due course. But I have come to inform you that meantime I have closed Lyng Park against all comers, including yourself."

"What? Good heaven, you cannot be serious!"

"Can I not? Do you suppose I tell you this for a joke?"

"But in that event no one can get to the church, not even myself — "

"Precisely, sir," Lord Langton said with the greatest satisfaction.

"But you can't do this, my lord," the Rector protested in dismay.

"Oh, but I can. There is no public right of way across my land from the village to the church. It is only by my kind permission that a right of way is granted, and now I have withdrawn that permission for the time being. The only ancient public right of way to the church is from the site of the old village that my great-grandfather pulled down, and that is within the park boundaries, and of no use to anyone except the deer."

"I never heard anything so shocking in my life," Mr Throckmorton muttered in a stunned voice. "You cannot keep people from divine worship."

"I can and I will. In any event, I dare say it is all for the best. Your church is scarce safe to stand up in."

"How dare you suggest such a thing, sir? You are merely making excuses for yourself as usual."

"Allow me to be a better judge of such matters than yourself, sir."

"I will not. The church is a trifle shabby, I'll own, and the roof leaks somewhat, but Miss Fenner-Smith has that all in hand now. She has started a fund for it, and in due course the repairs will be carried out."

"Have it your own way. It matters little to me. You can do nothing at present. The park remains closed till I find whoever was responsible for wrecking my gardens and damaging my pump-house. Any of my staff might have been killed. The whole house could have been burned down. As it is, every drop of water used will have to be carried from the pump in the stable yard."

"A great inconvenience to you, my lord, no doubt," Mr Throckmorton could not help saying sarcastically. "You fetch and carry all your own water, I am persuaded."

"Damn your insolence, sir! That is not what I meant. It is no hardship to me personally to use the pump, but it *is* a hardship for my staff, who have to cook and clean and wash, not to mention washing themselves. Do you see thirty or so servants all lining up for water at the yard pump?"

"Thus is man's frailty revealed when he puts his trust in man-made things," Mr Throckmorton murmured sadly.

"Confound your sermons, sir," Lord Langton cried furiously. "I have had a bellyful of them in the past and can stomach no more. Rather preach one to yourself about the sin of setting oneself above one's station. In future you will not make sheep's eyes at Lady Letitia Howard, nor will you entertain any notions of marrying her, for she is my ward and you are the last man on earth I'd let her marry. A penniless upstart of a parson who can't mind his own business and is prosing into the bargain."

Mr Throckmorton's pale young face had turned even paler, making the ugly purple bruise stand out more than ever.

"I have suffered much at your hands, my lord, but I will not suffer in silence being insulted to my face about my lowly state. There is no disgrace in being poor, sir, nor in being of low estate, and if you find me prosing I am sorry for it, for I mean not to be. I only say what I believe to be right. I know I have been acquainted with Lady Letitia only a short time, too short, you might think, to form any lasting attachment for her, but that is not so. I love her, and I believe she returns my sentiment, and I mean to marry her at any price, even if I have to wait till she is of age and free of your tyranny."

"My God, sir, were you not already

hurt I should knock you down again, for you richly deserve it for your impertinence. My sister is not yet eighteen, and would imagine herself in love with any young popinjay who made up to her and backed her up in her opposition to me. That is your sole purpose in pursuing her, is it not, to be revenged on me? Either that or to make a comfortable fortune for yourself. Perhaps both. Well, I will tell you straight, young man, you will never get a penny from her, for if by some mischance you do ever persuade her into a misguided alliance with yourself, I shall cut her off without so much as a bride dress."

"I should be glad for you to do so, my lord, for I want neither your money nor any part with you or your family, save Lady Letitia. You are not a fit or proper person to have the care of young people. You are heartless, tyrannical, and profligate, and — "

"And I trespassed on your meadow, is that it? Is that what rankles with you so?" Lord Langton bellowed at him.

"That is another matter entirely, and quite beside the point, though it is one

I wish to clear up once and for all with your lordship."

"This whole damnable business started merely because I expressed a desire to build an ornamental lake in my own park, and approached you in all common civility, about the possibility of diverting the river for that purpose across your meadow. For which rashness on my part, as it turns out, you have never since failed to abuse me, insult me, ridicule me, harass me at every point, and generally make me out some inhuman monster set on destroying everyone else for the mere furtherance of my own pleasure. Is there not some commandment about not maligning your neighbour? You would do well, Throckmorton, to go and preach yourself a sermon about it."

Sheldon paused to glare angrily at the Rector, who merely shrugged his shoulders and said calmly: "Indeed, you take me much amiss, my lord. But it was not only the matter of the river I referred to. It is your cruel injustice to Polly and your head groom. Perhaps with the man you had some slight justification, but with the girl, when 'twas you yourself got her with child — "

"And talking of James," the Marquis took him up, still in a towering rage, "where is the infernal fellow today?"

"Why, he has this very morning left for a post in Suffolk," Mr Throckmorton said in the greatest surprise.

"Precisely so. A strange coincidence, think you not, that he has so conveniently left the county the morning after my pump-house is destroyed?"

"What in the world are you saying, my lord?" Simon asked incredulously.

"I am not *saying* anything as yet, voicing an opinion merely. The fellow had cause enough to hate me, I'll confess, to wish to be revenged on me. You claim to stand up for the rights of your flock against my so-called tyranny. You know James is going away. He is conveniently resident here in your house, conveniently beholden to you, conveniently going away. What easier way for you to play tit-for-tat with me than by getting this man to do your dirty work for you by destroying *my* water supply before I get a supposed chance to destroy *yours*?"

The Rev. Mr Throckmorton was shocked into silence. Lord Langton lashed his riding boots with his whip with suppressed fury.

"*Well*?" he exploded at length.

"I can scarce believe my ears," Simon said quietly. "I never heard such libellous trash in all my life. For myself I care not a jot, but for James — He is an honest, hardworking fellow. 'Twould seem, my lord, wc are quite at a stand. There is no point my trying to talk with such a man as your lordship's self. You are only set on pursuing your own course, no matter who you harm."

"Oh, go to the devil, sir! You are nothing but a bigoted young jackanapes, not fit to be a parson. I am sick to death of you and your charades. But be warned, I shall get at the truth yet, and meanwhile the park remains closed. Good-day to you."

Lord Langton strode furiously from the Rectory, and rode back to Lyng House in the worst of bad moods.

9

FOR a couple of days there was
an uneasy kind of truce between
all opposing parties in New Lyng.
Lyng Park remained closed, to the fury
and frustration of the villagers and their
Rector in particular. At Lyng House the
Marquis supervised the repair work on
his pump-house that was going ahead
straight away, but otherwise did not stir
from his own front door. At night he
relieved his tensions in his latest fancy,
the new parlourmaid. At Roselands,
Josephine's condition became apparent
to her husband, and there was an
ensuing furious quarrel between them. At
the Rectory, the Rev. Mr Throckmorton
tried to compose his sermon for a service
he knew he would not be able to conduct,
owing to his inability to get to the church.
But he found that all he could think of
was Lady Letitia Howard, and wonder
how he could ever get to see her again.
His sermon became a letter to her

ladyship assuring her of his constant deep devotion to her and a promise that by hook or by crook he would see her again before too long. At Long Croft, Captain Fenner-Smith went right into his shell, daily awaiting with dread the expected arrival of his wife, and nursing a secret sense of guilt that he could voice to no one. His sister-in-law busied herself with organizing his domestic affairs, while his niece planned ways of raising money for the church fund, went shopping in Norwich for equipment for her Sunday School and its pupils, and wished she could stop thinking of Lord Langton and wondering how he did. At Lyng House Letty fretted and fumed at her brother's restrictions on her, but refrained from any childish display of temper in front of him, much to his surprise. No further sign of any activity on anyone's behalf was to be seen in the Rectory meadow.

To add to the anxieties of everyone there was a great uneasiness over the lack of cash about and the country bank notes being refused to be taken following the Bank of England's and all other Banks' stopping payment of cash. People were fearful of what would happen next, especially since many had very little cash to hand. It made their anger against Lord Langton's seeming selfish extravagance all the more intense. Meanwhile, the wind continued to howl about the countryside, gradually increasing in strength till it reached gale force.

Several times Sheldon went down to the church to see how it was standing up to the fury. He was dismayed but not surprised to note that several pieces of lead were ripped off the roof, but otherwise the building seemed fairly intact. If only the wind would soon abate, possibly no further damage would be done — this time!

But by the third day the gale was blowing stronger than ever, gusting across the countryside, bringing with it squalls of driving rain, bending the trees almost to the ground, sending giant waves crashing over the low coastline of North Norfolk, leaving a trail of havoc and debris in its wake. The waters of the little river Lyng began to rise alarmingly, and spread over the surrounding fields that bordered its banks. The people of New Lyng watched it warily. It frequently flooded to some extent, but only seriously once within living memory, and then with rather disastrous results, so the older inhabitants recalled. Meanwhile, everyone went about their daily business with heads bowed against the fury, hats crammed hard on heads, and clothes clasped tightly about bodies.

At the Rectory, Mrs Craske strongly advised young Mr Throckmorton to wear a flannel waistcoat and flannel drawers if he did not wish to catch cold in such dreadful weather, being as he wasn't used to such a bitterly cold, draughty climate. He thanked her kindly for her advice, but silently decided not to take it, at least till he was quite fifty years old.

At Long Croft Captain Fenner-Smith did succumb to a heavy cold, added to which his old wound started to play him up again, forcing him to take to his bed, to be fussed over by his anxious sister-in-law. At the same time Polly was taken bad, and seemed in danger of losing her child. Rosalind secretly cursed Lord Langton, took over the running of the house, and nursed Polly into the bargain.

At Roselands, Josephine, fast putting on weight, lost her looks and became peeky, irritable, and unwell. Roger Montagu decided he had had enough, and came to a decision. Accordingly he set out to brave the storms to ride to Lyng House.

At Lyng House, Letty tried to think how she could escape from her brother, just as soon as the gales died down. The Marquis, more restless than usual, wrapped himself in a heavy triple-caped greatcoat, crammed a low-crowned beaver hat on his head, and rode out at dusk to inspect the state of the slowly rising river. He rode across the open park, keeping clear of the trees as much as possible, for broken twigs and sticks were being whirled about, and even great branches were here and there wrenched off completely. The rain drove in his face, stinging his cheeks and eyes and making it almost impossible for him to see, while it was only his long experience in the saddle that enabled him to keep his seat and control his nervous mount.

The waters of the little Lyng, normally a clear, pretty stream flowing gently through idyllic pastures, were now swollen and muddy brown, swirling along at a great rate, carrying along twigs and dead leaves and various other flotsam. The rate at which it had risen was alarming. If it went any higher, it was in danger of flooding a great area of the low-lying part of the parish, where were situated several lonely farmsteads and cottages. If only it had been diverted across the Rectory meadow and into his proposed lake, the parish would have been safe, the excess water only going to raise the level of the lake. He had surmised that all along. Only now, with the results of his survey and in fact was he to be proved right. It was not he who would have caused the village to be flooded, but rather the opposite. His plans would have saved it. It was nature that was causing the flooding. Only everyone was so prejudiced against him, so gullible in listening to the Rector who knew nothing about the place, and their memories were short when it came to remembering floods of earlier years, that no one had believed him. Well, perhaps by morning they'd all wish they *had* listened to him.

As he turned to retrace his tracks home, he wrestled with his conscience. On the one hand, he told himself he ought to go and warn those in possible danger of what was happening. On the other, he reasoned, it was their own fault, no more than they deserved, he had been paid out for what he hadn't done, and it would serve them all right to suffer in their turn. The more vengeful side of his nature, which was usually uppermost, won, and, trying to close his mind to the consequences, he went back to Lyng House.

He was not best pleased on his return to discover that he had a visitor, especially since he had given strict orders for no one to be admitted through the gates who had not the business to be there. Casting off his dripping greatcoat and hat, Lord Langton swore violently at the footman who informed him of the visitor's presence in the library.

"God, the least you could do was make him wait in the Stone Hall, man," his lordship raged. "Who the devil is this pert and foolhardy fellow who forces his way in here and comes out on such a night to wait upon me?"

" 'Tis Mr Roger Montagu, milord, and we could not well say him nay. He's in rare high dudgeon."

"I see," Sheldon snapped, his voice and expression grim. "You may tell him I shall be with him shortly."

Having changed his clothes and fortified himself with brandy, so that he began to glow inside as he got warm again, Lord Langton finally went down to the library to face Mr Montagu. The older man was standing in front the fire, hands clasped behind his back, looking very ill-at-ease and embarrassed, his plump pink face pinker than usual with the cold and his efforts to buffet his way against the storm, the steam beginning to rise from his damp clothes. He was fast beginning to wish he had not come, particularly in such dreadful weather, but his whole future and that of his children was at stake, and having once got an idea into his mind he clung to it with the tenacity of the rather feeble-minded. Having got so far, he would not turn back now till he had accomplished his task.

"Good-evening, Montagu," the Marquis greeted him civilly if rather coldly. "This is a terrible night to be out visiting. You had as well stayed safe and snug by your own fireside in such inclement weather."

"This is not a social call, Langton," Mr Montagu returned, his voice a little high-pitched and petulant with the nervousness that was making him quake, but he was more determined than ever.

"Is it not?" Sheldon said, his tone perceptibly sharper. "I did not really suppose it could be. Might I then enquire the reason for this visit?"

"You may, sir. My wife, Lord Langton, is breeding again." Mr Montagu wondered at his own temerity.

"Am I then to congratulate you on the happy event?" Sheldon asked sarcastically.

"Your humour, sir, if so I take it to be, is a trifle misplaced in the circumstances, is it not, if you take my meaning?" the older man retorted, with even greater boldness.

"I beg your pardon," Sheldon said

stiffly, trying hard to keep his temper. "So of what are you accusing me? Pray have the goodness to tell me."

"You have seen much of Mrs Montagu of late, sir."

"I have seen much of a number of people of late, sir, too much, indeed. What does that signify?"

"Pray do not beat about the bush, Langton. You know what I mean."

"Rather it is you who are beating about the bush, sir," Sheldon said angrily, his temper flaring out of control. "What precisely *do* you mean?"

"I mean, my lord," Mr Montagu replied in a shaking voice, "that you have got my wife with child."

"Then pray be so good as to say what you mean, then we shall both know what we are talking about."

"I am persuaded, sir, you have known all along."

"You seem very anxious to lay her condition at my door, Montagu. Either you hold me in excessive dislike, and wish to raise a dust to discredit me, or else your imagination runs away with you. It is usual, is it not, to presume

261

that if one's wife is with child, the child is one's own?"

"I have not touched Mrs Montagu, Langton, for many a long month. In no way can the child she carries be my own. Whereas I know that you and she — It is my belief that she has already borne you one offspring, but as there could be no absolute certainty, I accepted the little one as mine. But that I am not prepared to do in the present circumstances. A man can take so much and no more."

"I see," Sheldon said, quietly once more, purposely avoiding Mr Montagu's accusing gaze. *Damn* Josephine for having deceived him so and brought him to such a pass, getting him in such a tight corner. What the devil was he supposed to say or do?

"You do not deny it, Langton?" the older man demanded in astonishment, as if half expecting he would.

"I do not, sir. To what purpose, pray?"

Mr Montagu stared at him, rather nonplussed.

"Well, is that all you have to say, confound you?" Sheldon cried irritably.

"What do you want me to do? Crawl on my bended knees and humbly crave your pardon?"

"That would not serve. What good would it do?"

"None. That is precisely my meaning. What's done is done. I make no excuses for myself, or for Josephine. I have never ever made much secret of the fact that she was my mistress. It was only out of respect for her wishes to spare your feelings that I have been as discreet as I have. Do you wish to call me out, is that it? If so, name your seconds, sir. It is not the first time I have been called to account in like circumstances." His hand automatically went up to the scar of his cheek, his long strong fingers briefly resting on the ugly little mark. It was one episode in his life that had nearly cost him much more than his honour. Was he prepared to pay the same price for Josephine? He knew in his heart he was not, but if called upon to do so he had little choice. He hadn't a leg to stand on. He was entirely at fault. Suddenly he found himself wishing Rosalind was there with him. He was

263

tired of fighting a constant battle of wills against all comers. Was there to be no peace or happiness in his life ever? But Miss Fenner-Smith would know what to say, what to do. She would soon put him to rights.

The thought of calling Lord Langton out had passed through Mr Montagu's mind, only to be cast aside as a last resort. He was no very good shot, he was not so young as he had been, and his sight was not so sharp. Besides, he had no wish to harm the young fellow, much as he disliked him. That would not solve anything.

"Demanding satisfaction of you, my lord," he said at length, very slowly, "much as I know I ought, would not bring me any happiness or peace of mind. I find I can no longer live with my wife's unfaithfulness. Therefore I ask that you take her into your care, and your child with her."

"Good God, you can't be serious!" Sheldon cried incredulously. "What an infernal notion! What on earth would I want with your wife?"

"What you have always wanted of

her, no doubt," Mr Montagu answered boldly.

"Confound your insolence, man!" the Marquis shouted angrily. "Keep your thoughts to yourself. I will have none of your wife, and that is final. Throw her out if you will, but do not look to me to take her in. She may walk the streets for all I care."

The words were spoken in anger, on the spur of the moment, and had he paused to examine them carefully he would have admitted that in all honesty he did not mean them, but Roger Montagu did not know this, and was apalled at the younger man's seemingly heartless cruelty.

"But your child, Langton — " he began.

"I want no part of it. The only children I want are those born of the woman I love, and since at present there is no such person — "

He broke off, the pain in his heart almost too much to bear. So much in his life these past twelve years Amelia was answerable for.

"I do not mean, Langton," Mr Montagu took him up, "that you should get away with this monstrous thing. You have behaved outrageously towards my wife and myself — ”

“And you mean to have retribution?” Sheldon said wearily.

“My wife has never been entirely faithful,” Mr Montagu blundered on. “I have ever known it so. She was expecting another man’s child when I married her. She was wed to me as a pure convenience on her side. But I loved her, and until you appeared on the scene we rubbed along pretty well together. I could overlook her little affairs as of no importance. But with you it has always been different with her. She has been as much in love with you as she ever will be with any man since the moment she first clapped eyes on you. That is why you have threatened myself and my family. I have known all along that she would leave me for you if ever she had the chance.”

“I am sorry. I had no notion,” Sheldon said, much shaken. “I fear I am not a very perceptive man. To me Josephine was just another woman, an excessively beautiful woman, but just a woman, nevertheless. It never entered my head

I was so playing with fire."

"Oh, the heedlessness of youth," Mr Montagu sighed sadly. "But it is too late for apologies now, young man."

"I cannot believe you would abandon your wife completely, sir," Sheldon said thoughtfully, regarding Mr Montagu's kindly, embarrassed pink face.

"I fear I cannot say the same of you, sir. I think you would leave her destitute."

Sheldon paced restlessly around the room, while out-side the rain pelted noisily against the windows like large peas ejected non-stop from a pea-shooter.

"Pray, give me time to think what is to be done," he said at length. "Your revelation puts an entirely different light on the matter. Unwittingly, perhaps, I seem to have led Josephine rather up the garden path. I must own myself quite put about. I scarce know whether I am on my head or my heels."

"If you have any honour, Langton — "

"I am as honourable as the next man, I trust," Sheldon broke in hotly.

"If you have any honour, sir," Mr Montagu went on firmly, "you will do what is right by Josephine. She is a lady of birth and breeding, not a serving maid to be cast aside and forgotten, with perhaps a paltry sum if she's lucky."

"I know it, but in all honesty, sir, I do not know what is to be done. I do not love her, and I certainly have no wish to live with her."

"You should have thought of that before you so heedlessly took your pleasure of her."

"I confess I have bungled the affair badly. But surely if you say you love her, can you not find it in your heart to forgive her and give her another chance? After this there can be nothing more between her and I."

"How very convenient for you such compliance on my part would be, would it not?" Mr Montagu retorted. "No doubt you took me for a doddering old fool, easy game for a lusty young jackanapes like yourself who wanted the pleasures of a woman without the responsibilities."

"That has always been my attitude to women since one particular woman used me ill years ago, but I never considered you at all."

"From what I hear, sir, that would appear to be your attitude to life. You consider no one but yourself."

Sheldon said nothing, suddenly remembering the rising waters of the river. God, what a bastard he was! If there was serious flooding, and anyone was hurt, or drowned, even, he would blame himself entirely, for letting his personal vengeance stand in the way of his public duty. Perhaps, after all, everyone else was right and he was wrong about himself. In that case even Amelia had been right. He was heartless and selfish and entirely self-centred, and deserved all he got.

Only what utter nonsense, he thought, with an abrupt change of attitude. One act of vengeance did not make him completely callous. This old fellow was playing on his sentiment to try and make him feel guilty about Josephine and take her in. And he would not do it. But the unaccountable thing was, he did feel guilty. He would have to do something for Josephine. He had already promised her he would not abandon her. In God's name, what was he to do? He sighed heavily.

"Go home, Montagu, pray do," he begged. "There is nothing to be gained from this conversation. You grow insulting, and I grow weary. I know I have landed myself in the devil's own mess. Only bear with me a while till I can see a way out of it. Let Josephine remain in your house a few days longer at least until I know what to do. I ask you of your charity."

"I have to go to town tomorrow for a few days. When I return, I shall not expect to find Mrs Montagu still in my house. I have told her as much."

Sheldon was about to retort that it was a heartless man who could turn a pregnant woman out-of-doors, but suddenly he remembered that it was precisely what he had done to Polly, the only difference being that Polly was only a serving wench and Josephine a lady of quality.

"Goodnight, Montagu," he said shortly, turning his back on his visitor.

"Goodnight, Langton," Mr Montagu mumbled, and hurried thankfully from the room.

Such an unpleasant interview, he thought, as he retrieved his hat and greatcoat from the footman and was shown out. It had cost him much soul-searching and sleepless nights to decide to come. Thank God it was now over, though he did not seem to have achieved much. Langton was such a very unpleasant young fellow to deal with. It was all such an unhappy coil. Would that he had never bought Roselands and thrown Josephine in the way of such a man.

As soon as he was out of the house, Mr Montagu had no chance for further reflection, being fully occupied with buffeting his way through the wildness of the night. His horse was nervous, and he had great difficulty in controlling it, or, indeed, in staying in the saddle at all. He did not get very far. A large branch being suddenly wrenched from one of the trees in the park right beside the carriageway, Mr Montagu's horse reared in panic and Mr Montagu was flung to the ground to lie motionless while his mount went careering off, riderless, into the night.

Meanwhile, Lord Langton sat sprawled in a chair beside the library fire, his feet stretched out to the blaze, a red-setter asleep on the rug beside him, the brandy decanter at his elbow. He was in a mood of black despair and self-pity. Montagu's visit had put him right out of humour. He did not want to be saddled with Josephine or her child. That was the main theme of his thoughts. And yet he had given her his word he would not abandon her, and he was a man of his word. If he lived with her, he could never marry her while she was tied to old Montagu, so she could never give him legal heirs. Not that he wanted to marry her, or live with her. He did not even want to keep her. She had deceived him. All women were deceivers. Except perhaps one, Rosalind Fenner-Smith. She was honest and spoke her mind, and if she often made him lose his temper and was uncomplimentary and sometimes downright rude to him, still he did not mind. He knew where he was with her, and she minded nothing he said or did. She could cope with everything. Even more important, she bore him no ill-will for anything. She merely accepted him as he was, and that was what no one had ever done before. Years ago, Amelia had hurt him so badly, had taken all the life and love out of his passionate youthful soul and left him cold and empty. Now this Rosalind Fenner-Smith, outrageous as she was, had struck a spark in the emptiness, and brought him the first glow of happiness he'd felt in years. But it was a spark he was almost afraid to fan into a flame, because he was afraid of getting burnt again. Even the one woman he had such a high regard for he did not entirely trust. But if anyone, she was the one he would wish to share his life with, given time to get to know her better, to let the wound in his heart heal. And now, when he had just found such a woman, here was Josephine come to threaten any chance of happiness he might have. Yet he knew Rosalind well enough to know that she would never countenance any kind of relationship with him if he did not do his duty by his ex-mistress, yet if he did his duty, he would not be in a position to make an honourable proposition to any other woman. It was all an infernal web in which he suddenly found himself enmeshed. Of course, he could set Josephine up in a house of her own, but he did not think that would suit her, especially if, as her husband maintained, she entertained some deeper feeling for him. He was well acquainted with her and her ways. She would give him no peace, would torment him and pursue him in an endeavour to regain his favours.

And that was one thing he would never do again, he resolved. He would never touch Josephine Montagu again. Right now he felt he never wanted to touch any woman again, except perhaps Miss Smith. And he knew he could well do without women if he so wished. He had the willpower to do so. He had been completely faithful to Amelia during the whole time of their courtship and engagement, even though he'd had women enough before. Not many men could boast such fidelity. It was only since she'd jilted him that he'd made no attempt to restrain his natural desires. But with the right woman he would be faithful always.

He finished the brandy, and began on gin. The embers of the fire died down. Outside, the terrific storm reached its peak. Lord Langton slowly and deliberately drank himself into a stupor. Finally he fell into a deep sleep, the dog faithfully stretched out beside him.

In the cold light of dawn, the storm at last blew itself out. The red-setter woke up and barked at his master to be let out. Bleary-eyed, Sheldon gradually came to. The room spun. His head ached violently, and he felt exceedingly sick. He shivered. The fire was quite gone out, only a heap of greyish white ash in the hearth. The empty decanters beside him told their own story. The first thing that struck him was the silence. No wind howling, no rain beating against the windows, no storm at all raging. Only a great hush. Till the dog barked again, going to the door and whining and scratching to get out.

"Me, too, old fellow," Sheldon told him, making an effort to get to his feet. He staggered a little, and clutched at the chair back. The dog barked impatiently, and rather sleepily he trod across the room and opened the door. The animal went scampering on ahead. More slowly, Lord Langton made his way to the lavish crested water closet he had installed off the Stone Hall. A couple of maids, busily scrubbing the black and white tiled floor, were completely taken aback at sight of him, for though in general he was an early riser, he was never abroad quite so early, especially bleary-eyed and unshaved, his hair untidy, his clothes crumpled and his cravat half undone, and altogether looking as if he had been hitting the bottle rather hard. They stopped their giggling and working at once, and turned to bob him a respectful if astonished curtsy. But he did not seem to notice them and merely went on his way.

Having answered the call of nature, and managed to fight back the rising nausea, he felt a little better, and, still in rather a daze, half stumbled and half walked down the stairs after the dog to the South Door. The fresh cold morning air hit him like a douche of icy water. The shock sobered him at once. The great dark night clouds were rolling back to leave a widening expanse of brilliant silvery sky swept clean by the recent storms. He blinked in the glare. The close-mown greenness of the grass, still dim in the dawn light, and glistening with raindrops, stretched away seemingly endlessly. The dog bounded off eagerly to attend to its business. Sheldon remained where he was, taking in great breaths of keen air, and admiring the beauty of the prospect before him. Evidence of the storm was strewn all about: one or two smashed slates off the roof, twigs and branches and dead leaves, bits of household debris from the kitchen wing. His immediate thoughts were of the river Lyng and the church. Had there been any serious flooding while he had been in a deliberately self-inflicted drunken stupor? How had the church stood up to the torment?

He strolled across the gravel path and over the grass a little way, then turned round to look back and up at the great square Palladian house with its four cupolas in each corner and its elegantly curving colonnaded wings. With some dismay he noted that the weathervane on one of the cupolas had been stripped away. Doubtless there was much more damage about the estate. He would have to go round with his steward to discover the precise extent of it. But first he must find out what had happened to the river and the church.

He whistled, and the red-setter came bounding back to him, leaping excitedly round him, and bestowing wet if loving kisses on his hands. He fondled the creature affectionately, then went indoors again.

Half an hour later, once more his usual elegant, immaculate self, Lord Langton entered the breakfast room, but he could only manage a cup of coffee, for one thing because his stomach still felt decidedly queasy, and the sight of food made him want to throw up, for another because he was so impatient to ride out to inspect the storm damage. But he found his senses were still reeling, and all he could do was remain sitting at the table with his throbbing head in his hands. However, the Most Noble Marquis of Langton was noted for the hardiness and physical fitness on which he prided himself, many a sturdy fellow going under the table or being knocked up long before his lordship. Now he made a very determined effort, and soon managed to overcome his feelings, and make his way to the stables, having first issued strict orders that his steward was to join him there directly, even if it meant dragging the man out of his bed.

Fortunately for the steward, since he did not want to incur his lordship's displeasure or, even worse, dismissal, he was already up and about, and was able to obey his summons at once. As he went to the stables, he found Lord Langton already in the saddle, impatient to be off.

"Good-morning, Oakley," Sheldon said shortly. "I am glad you have not kept me waiting above a few minutes. I don't pay you to lie in bed of a morning."

"No, my lord, I understand that," Oakley returned respectfully.

Oakley, who, though an astute, hard-working steward, was not as young as he had been, and had put on considerable weight with the years, had hoped that his lordship, judging by the looks of him, for he had obviously been drinking hard, thus his haggard appearance, would have been a trifle slower than usual. He was disappointed though perhaps not very surprised to find that my lord was as full of restless energy as ever. Without more ado, he whirled his horse about and rode at a gallop out of the stable-yard, leaving Oakley to follow at a more sedate pace on his elderly cob.

Even the fate of the church was forgotten in Sheldon's anxiety to get to the river to find out the result of something he had fast come to consider his fault. Ignoring fallen branches and uprooted trees, he careered headlong across the park, the sharp air stinging his cheeks and making the blood race in his veins. He forgot all about Oakley, who was left far behind.

The light was stronger now, though the first brilliance of daybreak had faded. Despite the cold, there was a lift of spring in the air. Even this did not distract Lord Langton from the one thought in his mind. He took the fence that separated the park from the lane at a flying leap, knowing no fear and confident in his own ability and judgement. He did not slacken his pace in the lane, but went racing along, splashing heedlessly through the puddles, the hooves of his horse sending wet mud flying up in all directions. Only when he came to the low-lying meadows by the river did he slow down, and then he drew rein in dismay.

"Oh God!" he exclaimed aloud.

For where before there had been merely rather boggy fields with a swollen brown river flowing through them, there was now a wide expanse of flat and placid water reflecting the translucent sky, with here and there a stark skeleton of a tree sticking up out of it, and one or two half-submerged houses. An improvised raft made out of an upturned door, bearing some three or four people, was being paddled unsteadily across the unnatural sea. Even as Sheldon watched in fascinated horror, the frail craft capsized, throwing its occupants into the water, where they floundered desperately, frantically waving their arms about and trying to clutch at twigs.

Sheldon was thankful then for hardy boyhood days when he and other young lads had swum naked in the creeks and inlets along the North Norfolk coast at Blakeney and Wells. He was as strong and accomplished a swimmer as he was a horseman. Throwing off his coat and hat, he plunged into the water and struck out towards the struggling unfortunates. Luckily three of them had managed to grab hold of the door, and were clinging on to it for dear life. The fourth one had already gone under a couple of times and bobbed up again in a vain attempt to stay afloat. Sheldon reached him as he went down for the third time. He caught hold of him, and, breathing rather heavily, dragged him to the shore in safety. Dumping his dripping burden there, he then swam back to help the others clamber back on their raft. With one less person on it, it was easier to manoeuvre, and some while later all three were on dry land.

By this time Oakley, very much astonished, had arrived on the scene. A dripping Lord Langton was already back in the saddle, wheeling his horse about.

"Look to them, man," he ordered his steward sharply. "Take them back to Lyng House and see they are fed and dried."

He was gone before Oakley had a chance to reply.

Hardly conscious of his drenched clothes clinging uncomfortably to his skin, Sheldon headed back towards the church. He expected the worst, and was not spared. The sight that met his eyes grieved him far more than the flooded river had done. The tower still stood intact, but half the leads from the nave roof had been stripped away, the roof of the chancel had fallen in completely at one end, and the large stained glass window behind the altar had blown in. The debris was strewn all about the churchyard among the tombstones and ancient yew trees. Sheldon could only stare at it in the greatest dismay, till he became aware that he was shivering with cold, and could hardly stop his teeth from chattering.

Slowly now, with one last look at the devastated little church, he turned and rode back to Lyng House.

10

FROM one of the glass window embrasures of the gallery above the Stone Hall, Lady Letitia Howard watched Mr Montagu being escorted across the Hall and into the library. Full of curiosity, wondering what Josephine's husband could be doing paying a call on such a wild night, Letty remained where she was, pressed up against the opening as unobtrusively as possible. Her patience was eventually rewarded when she heard a brisk, angry step on the tiled floor far below, and her brother appeared, his scowl more pronounced than usual, and vanished into the library.

Silently Letty flitted down the stairs, her slight figure mingling with the shadows in the corners where the brilliant light of the myriad candles in the great brass chandelier did not reach. There was no one about in the Stone Hall. Feeling rather guilty at spying on her brother, sure Mr Throckmorton would not approve, but feeling justified in the circumstances, she stationed herself outside the library door and bent her head to the keyhole. She could not catch all that was being said, but could hear enough to know that Mr Montagu had come to call her brother to account for getting Josephine with child. Well, serve him right, she thought. He deserved all he got. Then it struck her that Mr Throckmorton would not consider that a very charitable notion, and hurriedly changed her mind. In all honesty, she had to admit that Sheldon always did what he believed was right, even if it wasn't. He had always done what he thought best for her, even if she hadn't agreed with him. He had been her protector and mentor, the supplier of all she had, since their mother's death when she was a few months old. She didn't really wish him any harm, only wished he would be more tolerant, less ill-tempered. Deep down in her heart, she knew she loved him, but she did not actually *like* him. There was a vast difference between the two.

She suddenly wanted to giggle, though it was more from nerves than mirth.

Poor Sheldon, to be given such a raking down like an errant schoolboy by old Mr Montagu. How humiliating! He *did* deserve it, but even so — And just supposing Mr Montagu called him out, and, unlikely as it seemed, just supposing he got hurt or, worse still, *killed*! The thought was too horrible. It was not likely to happen, but it was always a possibility. Years ago, when she was a child of ten, Sheldon had been called out by just such an irate husband. She was not supposed to have known anything about it, but servants gossiped, and an inquisitive little girl could not help overhearing. Anyway, even Sheldon himself could not hide the ugly red gash on his cheek where the ball had grazed his face. He bore the mark to this day. But she had been frightened for him then, and she felt uneasy for him now. He had stirred up so much anger and hatred against himself of late. The sabotaging of the pump-house had made her really angry on his behalf, though she had not let him know it. He was, after all, her only brother, and she owed him some family allegiance.

At the same time, though, he had

used her in an excessively high-handed manner, keeping her a virtual prisoner since her return from the Rectory, and absolutely forbidding her to see Mr Throckmorton. It was all because of this stupid feud between them over the river. Otherwise she was sure even Sheldon could not fail to like Mr Throckmorton, for he was the dearest, kindest man conceivable, and in his turn would doubtless try and like Sheldon out of Christian charity. In any event, she meant to see him again, whatever her brother said. And now, under cover of darkness and the fury of the storm, while Sheldom was occupied with Mr Montagu, might be the best time.

Suddenly determined to carry out her hastily devised scheme, Letty hurried away to get ready.

★ ★ ★

Josephine, sitting alone at Roselands, heard her husband go out and wondered what the consequences of his visit to Lord Langton would be. She had been feeling alternately sick and dizzy all day, and only dogged determination had kept her from her bed. She would not let anyone have the satisfaction of crowing over her condition. That she could not bear. It would be the last straw. She was a proud woman, and the public shame she soon seemed like to be called on to bear would be torture enough. Private shame, from those who knew her intimately, struck her as so much worse.

She realized now what a complete and utter fool she had made of herself over Sheldon Howard, had let her heart rule her head, and now here she was pregnant with a child she did not want, a child *he* did not want, and like to be thrown into the street by her outraged husband. She would lose everything she had, her home, her children, her good name, her self-respect, even. And for what? For a man who cared not a fig for her, who had taken her as he had taken Polly the chambermaid, to pick up and put down when he tired of her, or when she became an inconvenience or an encumbrance to him. She had gambled her all to try and win him, and had lost miserably.

She cringed every time she thought of the way she had pleaded with him not to abandon her. How she had debased herself! Like some cheap little street girl begging for mercy from her seducer. It was all so humiliating. No man was worth such a price.

Especially a man like Sheldon Howard. Her eyes had been opened at last. He was quite without heart or sensibility, a man devoted entirely to gratifying his own whims and desires at the expense of everyone else. Why in heaven's name had she not been content with her gentle, kindly, easy-going husband who, if he was comfortable like an old pair of slippers, at least loved her? Or had once. God, she had not known when she was well off. What she would not give now to regain that love, that peace and security and harmony of the earlier days of their marriage before she had met Lord Langton. If only she could turn the clock back, be given a second chance, she would try and be a good wife and mother and forget the Marquis. The love of a good and honest man was worth far more than a few hours forbidden pleasure in bed with a callous lecher, however exciting and expert a lover he might be, and that there was no denying Sheldon was. Well, she had had her excitement with him, and now she had had her fill of it.

Even now she could scarce believe that Mr Montagu would throw her out, would leave her to the mercy of a man who had none. He had said he did not want to find her in his house when he returned from town, did not want to see her ever again. She could scarce believe that either. Where was she to go, what was she to do? He had not even said he would provide for her. And she felt so bad she did not feel like going anywhere.

Still thinking along these lines, she finally dozed off by the fire, while the fury of the storm outside gathered to its peak.

She was awakened much later by her maid gently shaking her.

"Ma'am, Mr Montagu has not yet returned. I think you should go to bed."

"I dare say he is sheltering from the storm," she said, trying to sound cheerful. "It is getting worse, I vow."

"Indeed, yes, ma'am. But you won't wait up for the master, will you, ma'am?"

"No, Tucker, I will not. Come, help me to bed."

Josephine went to bed, but she did not sleep. She lay for hours in the darkness, listening to the raging torment outside, wondering what would come of her, what had happened at Lyng House, why Mr Montagu had not returned, while every now and again violent pains in her stomach nearly doubled her up with their intensity.

Towards morning she finally slept, only to awake an hour later screaming hysterically with pain. At the same time Mr Montagu was being brought indoors on a stretcher. He was unconscious, suffering from exposure, and appeared to have sustained a severe blow on the head, possibly from his horse's flailing hooves. A few hours later, Josephine Montagu miscarried of the child she was expecting.

* * *

At the Rectory, the Rev. Mr Simon Throckmorton, too, sat listening to the storm. He could not rest easy, for, like Lord Langton, he was anxious about the rising river and the state of the church. Unlike Lord Langton he did not have either of these things on his conscience. He heard one of his chimney-pots come crashing down outside, which so frightened the maids that they set up a terrified screaming, and he had to leave his fireside to go and comfort them. Even Mrs Craske was so alarmed, convinced the end of the world had come, that she refused to go back to her own room. So he sat up in the kitchen with them, drinking tea and reading comforting words from the Bible. He was thus employed when a frantic knocking on the front door was heard. He himself, in great astonishment, went to answer it, and was even more astonished when a dripping, exhausted figure shrouded in a voluminous cloak and hood almost fell into the hall.

Once inside, the figure threw back the hood, and the pale, frightened face of Lady Letitia Howard was revealed.

"Oh, thank heaven I have got here!" she gasped. "I had no notion the storm was so violent, else I had not set out in the first place. I was so terrified. I could scarce stand, and was in the greatest dread every moment of a tree falling on me."

"My dear Lady Letitia," Mr Throckmorton said kindly and gently, "whatever prevailed upon you to venture out on such a night? Does your brother know you are here?"

"Sheldon? Good gracious, no! He would be so angry. Pray do not tell him, sir. He is closeted with Mr Montagu, discussing a *very delicate matter*. So I took the opportunity to slip out unobserved."

"My dear young lady, of course I shall not tell him," Mr Throckmorton assured her. Now that he was suddenly face to face with this young woman he had dreamed of for so many days and nights, he was overcome with embarrassment, and knew not what to say. Not so her ladyship who, having safely attained her goal, was fast recovering her usual spirits.

"You see, I had to escape from Lyng House," she explained, the damp brown curls bobbing excitedly round her animated little face. "My brother has absolutely forbidden me to see you again, and Miss Fenner-Smith was going to accompany me to wait upon you, to make it all terribly proper, only she has been so busy running the house, as her uncle was taken ill, and nursing that odious Polly, and running round all over the place for everyone, that she never had time to come with me. So I realized I must make shift for myself, or I should never see you again. You can have no idea how unhappy your stupid feud with Sheldon has made me."

"I am very sorry for it — " Mr Throckmorton began.

"You might have killed each other that night in the meadow. It really is too bad in you both. I *wish* you will stop. You know, my brother is not such a dreadful ogre as you might think. He is even quite *nice* sometimes, though not very often. Cannot you sort this whole wretched business out between you in a civilized manner, so that you and I can be more comfortable together?"

"Indeed, my lady, I wish I might,"

Simon said fervently. "Nothing would make me happier. But Lord Langton, I fear, will not heed a word I say. And though I am prodigious happy to see you, really you ought not to have come, alone, on a night like this, against your brother's wishes and without even his knowledge. It is highly improper, besides you might have been injured in the storm. When your brother finds out you are here — Well, my dear, think you it will make him look any more kindly on any case?"

"Oh dear, no, it will not," she said in distress. "I had not thought of that. Truly, I am very sorry. Only I was so anxious to see you — "

"Pray do not take on so, ma'am. You are here now, and I cannot possibly permit you to go out again in this storm. You will have to remain here till the morning. Mrs Craske will care for you. Oh dear, I dare say Lord Langton will very likely call me out for this night's work."

"Oh, no! Surely even Sheldon could not be so idiotish as that. It is not as if I had spent the night actually *with* you."

"That makes little difference in the circumstances, I fear. Never mind, it is too late for regrets now. Come into the parlour and take off your wet cloak, and warm yourself by the fire there. Mrs Craske will get you a hot drink in no time at all."

So Letty sat by the roaring fire in the shabby parlour at the Rectory, drinking hot chocolate, and wearing a pair of Mr Throckmorton's old slippers, which were many sizes too large for her, for she had walked all the way from Lyng House and her own shoes were soaked through. But to her chagrin she sat alone, for Mr Throckmorton was too nice in his sentiments, and would not take advantage of the situation to deliberately go against her brother's wishes and pursue his courtship of her. Much as he loved and wanted to marry her, as far as he was concerned, Lord Langton was her legal guardian, and as such, no matter his own differences with his lordship, he respected the older man's wishes with regard to his sister. The Rector was too honourable to do otherwise, and Letty, thinking on the matter, knew in her heart that really she would not have it any other way.

Several times throughout the long evening, Mr Throckmorton came into the parlour to see how she did, and finally, towards ten o'clock, to inform her that Mrs Craske had made up the bed in the guest chamber for her, and put a warming-pan in it, and she could sleep there. He trusted she would be comfortable and sleep well, and he would escort her back to Lyng House first thing in the morning. He then bid her goodnight and God bless. But the way he said it and the look he gave her made her heart sing, and she went happily to bed knowing that indeed she had found a good man who loved her and whom she loved in return.

It was in the small hours of the morning that the whole household was woken up by men from the village to inform the Rector that the river had broken its banks and flooded the surrounding countryside for the distance of a mile or more, and that help was needed. The gates of Lyng House being firmly shut, no one was going to go there begging for help, so all the help they could get was required.

Leaving his womenfolk in the care of Mrs Craske, the Rector and his menservants joined forces with other men from the village and sallied out to see what was to be done to rescue those affected by the rising flood.

★ ★ ★

Arriving back at Lyng House, tired, wet, cold, shivering, and very dispirited, Lord Langton was greeted with the news that Lady Letitia was missing. Her bed had not been slept in, there was no note or anything of that nature from her, and she had not been seen since last evening. To Sheldon it was the final blow. He groaned aloud, and the servants that knew him well thought they had never seen him look so troubled. A lesser man might have burst into tears. But the Marquis of Langton had not cried since his mother had died seventeen years ago. Even Amelia had not been able to break him completely. He issued strict orders that her ladyship must be searched for immediately, then he went up to his room to dry off and change.

As soon as that was done, he went straight down to the estate office to find Oakley. His steward had just come in, and was sitting at his desk looking rather fatigued.

"Well, man?" Lord Langton demanded sharply.

"Er-well, what, my lord?" Oakley mumbled, feeling quite incapable of coping with his employer's short temper after such an ordeal as he had just been through.

"For heaven's sake, man, I presume you have not just returned from a picnic, have you?" Langton snapped back at him sarcastically. "I mean, have you attended to the poor devils from the flood?"

"Yes, my lord. The housekeeper herself is giving them breakfast right now."

"Good. Now, pray do not loll about like that, Oakley. You have much to attend to. Firstly, the church has suffered excessive damage. Half the chancel roof has fallen in, besides much else. I want you to have full repairs put in hand at once, d'you understand? No expense is to be spared. I will bear the full cost myself."

"Very good, my lord," the steward said, in some bewilderment, wondering if he had heard aright. What sudden change of heart was this in his lordships?

"Secondly," Lord Langton went on, striding up and down the office in his impatient, restless way, "I want any damage done by the flood, no matter to whose property, made good at my expense. Is that clear?"

"Yes, my lord," Oakley murmured, in even greater bewilderment. "Is that all?"

"All? Good God, man, what more do you want, pray? Is that not enough to be going on with?"

"Yes, my lord."

"Then be getting on with it."

"Very good, my lord."

Sheldon turned and abruptly strode from the room, leaving a bemused steward to wonder what maggot had got into his noble employer's head.

Lord Langton, meanwhile, had only one thing in mind: to find Letty, and quite suddenly it had come to him where she might be. The Rectory. Why had he not thought of that before?

Still full of the same restless energy,

Sheldon went at once to the stables, ordered the black mare to be saddled, and was soon off at a great rate down the back drive to the Rev. Mr Throckmorton's house. It was still comparatively early, and he did not know if the Rector would be abroad yet, but if not he was determined to drag him from his bed to speak with him.

The homely red-brick Rectory stood peacefully in the middle of lawns alight with long fingers of pale wet morning sunshine. Throckmorton might be poor, Sheldon thought, but he kept his house and garden clean and tidy, particularly his garden. It bore the mark of a garden lover like himself. But if the impertinent young jackanapes thought to abduct and compromise Letty, he had another think coming.

Leaving his horse tethered in the lane, Lord Langton strode up the garden path and rapped impatiently on the front door. When a rather scared looking Mrs Craske answered it, he did not pause to enquire if her master was at home, but brushed past her into the hall, saying shortly:

301

"Inform your master I am here. I wish to see him at once, if you please."

"Very good, my lord," the housekeeper returned respectfully, thinking what a very unfortunate manner the young man had.

Mr Throckmorton, however, had already heard his lordship's voice in the hall, and now emerged hurriedly from the breakfast room with his napkin still tucked in the front of his shirt. He looked so ludicrous that Sheldon almost laughed in his face, but inherent good breeding prevented him from doing so. Instead he said more politely:

"I am sorry to interrupt your breakfast, Throckmorton, but there is a matter I wish to discuss with you."

"Of course, my lord," Simon said hastily. "Pray come into my study. This way, if you please."

"Do you usually receive visitors with your napkin tucked in your front?" Sheldon asked, not unkindly, as he followed the Rector down the hall.

The young man blushed scarlet, and snatched the napkin away.

"I beg your pardon, my lord," he said

stiffly. "I meant no offence. I was not aware — "

"Pray do not apologize to me, young man. It is of no consequence to me if you are in your nightshirt. I have more important things to concern myself with. Such as where is my sister?" His eyes narrowed as he saw the Rector's expression change. He added astutely: "I perceive by your look that you know something of the matter."

"She is still sound asleep upstairs in my guest chamber," Simon admitted, half apologetic, half rueful. "She is not harmed at all."

"Thank God she is safe, at all events," Sheldon said fervently, too relieved to be angry.

"I was going to escort her home as soon as she is up," Mr Throckmorton went on hurriedly. "You must believe me, my lord, when I say that she came here without any knowledge or encouragement on my behalf. I have not laid a finger on her."

"I did not suppose you had," his lordship said drily. "You are, after all, a man of the cloth."

"You once said, my lord," Mr Throckmorton reminded him, still with heightened colour, "that I was not fit to be a parson."

"I have a hasty temper, sir, and often say a number of things I do not mean," Sheldon explained, with a faint rather amused smile. "I am rather better acquainted with my sister than you, and can well believe she devised some madcap scheme to come and see you. Though I must confess I did at first think perhaps you had abducted her with a mind to putting her in a compromising situation. But I realize now how nonsensical that notion is."

"Thank you, my lord," Mr Throckmorton said quietly. "Believe me when I say I have your sister's well-being at heart. I hold her in the highest regard. I would not do anything to jeopardize my chances of eventually marrying her."

"You really believe I will let *you* marry my sister?" Sheldon cried incredulously. "Do you not realize how far above you in birth and wealth she is?"

"Yes, my lord, but still I hope. I do not condemn her for her birth and wealth."

"You do not condemn her? By God, that's rich!" Lord Langton gave one of his unexpected loud shouts of laughter. "So you would not object to being related to the wicked Marquis of Langton, eh?"

"I would put up with anything to have the honour of having her as my wife, sir, but I do not have any great hope of that till she is of age."

"Do you not, indeed? Most wise in you, considering the circumstances. Do you not realize my sister could marry almost anyone in the land?"

"Yes, my lord, but I do not believe she wishes to."

"You think she really cares for you?" Sheldon asked in surprise. "You have known each other such a little while, and she is very young."

"Long enough, sir, and she is quite old enough. My mother was only seventeen when she wed my father."

"If you are genuinely attached to each other, I will engage not to stand in your way. I suffered enough myself from affairs of the heart years ago. I would not have it happen to my little sister. You must prove your regard for her."

Mr Throckmorton was staring at the older man in disbelief.

"I am persuaded you might be a calming influence on my sister," Langton went on. "At present she flies up into the bows at the least little provocation. I fancy she will not do that often with you. How she will take to the life of a poor country Rector's wife in a shabby rectory I know not, after the life she has been accustomed to at Lyng House, but that is your problem. If she does indeed care enough for you — "

"I presume to believe so."

"Then you have my permission to pay court to her, though I will not allow her to wed till she is eighteen."

"Thank you, sir. I am indeed most happy and obliged to you," Mr Throckmorton murmured, quite overcome.

"Oh, don't do it too brown," Sheldon said, somewhat impatiently.

"But there is still a matter between us — " the Rector began awkwardly.

"The river? Yes, I know it. And I think you will find the matter has resolved itself. You are aware the river flooded in the night?"

"Yes, yes. I have been up half the night helping the poor souls who were flooded out. A terrible business, to be sure."

"Four you overlooked. I found them struggling to get to safety on a raft improvised from a door. Unfortunately it capsized and tipped them all into the water. But luckily I am a strong swimmer, and was able to be of some assistance to them."

"*You*, my lord?" the Rector's astonishment was great.

Sheldon raised a quizzical dark brow. He said in a quelling manner:

"So surprised? Have I not always told you I am not an inhuman monster? Did you suppose I would stand by and let them drown? But that is neither here nor there, sir. The thing is, if only you had not been such a pig-headed nincompoop and had listened to me in the first place, all this trouble would have been avoided. If only you had let me divert the river, it would not have flooded. Instead the excess water would all have been taken up by my ornamental lake. Perhaps not so ornamental after all, I might suggest. I know this for a scientific fact. When you

307

caught me trespassing on your land, I was having a survey done to prove my theory. I was *not* trying to carry out my wicked plans by stealth, as you and everyone else believed. I am neither such a fool nor so malicious."

"Then why did you not tell me — " Mr Throckmorton began in considerable embarrassment.

"Because, my dear young man, you would not listen. You were so prepared to think the worst of me always, that I gave up wasting my breath. Perhaps it was wrong in me, but I demean myself to no one, and was prepared to let you think what you liked of me, rather than beg you to heed my point of view. That is another unfortunate failing of mine you must learn to live with if ever you become my brother-in-law. However, I *was* wrong in the stand I took over the church, as a result of which it has suffered very severe damage from the storm. I should not have made it a point of issue between us. I hope I make amends by undertaking to repair the fabric throughout thoroughly at my own expense. I have already instructed my steward to put the matter in hand."

"I know not what to say, my lord," Mr Throckmorton said, quite bereft of words.

"Furthermore," Lord Langton continued, as if he had not heard, "to prove I bear my neighbours and tenants no ill-will, I will engage to assist anyone who suffers difficulties over shortage of cash through this crisis with the Banks. Perhaps then you will not preach sermons against me about its being easier for a camel to pass through the eye of a needle than for a rich man to enter the kingdom of heaven. You may have thought I was asleep, but I assure you I was not. I heard every word."

"I beg your pardon. A most unfortunate choice of subject. Most remiss of me — "

"No matter. I dare say it did me no harm. The thing is, will you now let me go across your meadow with my scheme? You have my solemn oath no one will suffer by it, else I should not go ahead with it. Indeed, I design to improve the village water supply. My great-grandfather made New Lyng a model village. It deserves a model water supply."

Mr Throckmorton gaped. He did not know what to say. He could hardly believe this was the same man as the one he had come to blows with in his meadow that unfortunate night, the same one he had been at daggers drawn with for so long. Yet so it was. What made a man change so overnight? Or was it he, Simon Throckmorton, who had been grossly mistaken in the Marquis? He doubted if he would ever know the answer.

"You will have to go to authorities higher than my own, my lord, it being church land, but I will no longer oppose your scheme. I am only too happy to have our differences so amicably resolved at last. You can have no notion how it has worried me and robbed me of my sleep. I simply did not know how to cope with the situation, I must confess."

"Only pray do not preach at me any more. Nothing sets my back up quicker. Here, my hand on it, sir. I trust we shall go on better together in future." He held out his hand to the younger man, his face brightened by one of his rare smiles as he did so. With an answering smile on his own serious young countenance, Simon too held out his hand, and the two shook hands cordially.

"I will leave Letty to you to bring home in your own good time," Sheldon went on, still smiling. "I do not want my shins kicked for my efforts."

"And you will not now pursue James about sabotaging your pump-house?" the Rector cried eagerly.

"What, will you have your pound of flesh even now?" my lord demanded with fast rising anger. Then, at Mr Throckmorton's hurt look, he laughed out loud again, and said reassuringly: "No, I will not pursue the matter now, sir. I have no proof against him. Let him go and all well and good. I cannot really believe he was responsible for such an act."

"And Polly, my lord — "

"Pray don't goad me too far, sir," Langton cut him short in dangerous tones. "Polly is quite a different kettle of fish. She sought to give herself airs and graces because she had been to my bed, and that does not do in a servant. I would have sent her packing in the circumstances, in any event. A good servant would have rejected my advances in the first place. Any who do not I do not want to remain in my service after. Am I not right?"

"It is an odd way of regarding the matter," Mr Throckmorton spoke up boldly, "and I cannot agree with you upon it, but I have no wish to fall out with you over it. Polly is in good hands at Long Croft, and is indeed fortunate to have a mistress like Miss Fenner-Smith to nurse her during her time."

"*Nurse* her?" Lord Langton roared furiously. "What the devil are you talking about, man? Do you tell me Miss Smith is *nursing* a former doxy of mine?"

"I believe the girl was taken bad, my lord. What else would you have Miss Fenner-Smith do?"

"I won't *have* it," Sheldon cried, in rare high dudgeon. "Polly is a baggage. Miss Smith is a lady. More than that, she is a *saint*."

"Precisely, my lord," Mr Throckmorton said with satisfaction, feeling his lordship had trapped himself with his own words. But, it suddenly struck him, why was the Most Noble Marquis of Langton so concerned for the Captain's very plain niece? Could it be that — No, never. Such a thing was quite out of the question. Such a man could never fall for such a woman. And yet stranger things had been known to happen. "Perhaps, my lord," Simon ended, very respectfully, "you should tell Miss Fenner-Smith herself, not me."

"By God, Throckmorton, you're right. I will." All at once Sheldon remembered Josephine, and knew that he had no right to tell Rosalind anything, least of all how he felt about her. He turned away bleakly. Not only Amelia to torment him now, but Josephine as well. Lord, what he wouldn't do to be back amongst the ancients of Greece and Egypt, but with Napoleon stampeding all over Europe, there was no escape anywhere. "Good-day, sir," he ended flatly, his rage quite gone. "Pray have a care of my sister for me, and do not worry overmuch about your church. I have re-opened Lyng Park."

"Good-day, my lord, and thank you."

Lord Langton left a bemused young Rector to break the good news of her brother's blessing to Lady Letitia.

Sheldon rode slowly home, matching his pace to his mood. He tried to imagine what it would be like to go home to Josephine and her squalling brat, and shied away from the thought. The prospect held no joy for him. He did not even desire her body any more. How then could he ever live with her? Even had he not met Miss Smith, he doubted if he would have wanted Josephine any longer. He was beginning to tire of her before ever she was with child. If only he had broken free of her then. But she had become almost a habit, she'd been his mistress so long, and she had clung to him so. Now, too late, he knew why. God, how he'd bungled things of late!

His first thought on reaching home was for food. He had regained his appetite by now, and was ravenously hungry. So he sat down to a solitary late breakfast, feeling very depressed and sorry for himself. Shortly after that, Letty came home, in great spirits, to throw her arms round her brother, and declare he was quite the best brother in the world, she loved him for ever, and she was sorry she had ever thrown her dinner at him. All of which cheered Sheldon so much that he quite forgave her for running off, without so much as a scold, and suggested that they go to Norwich for a couple of days together, do some shopping, perhaps go to the Theatre Royal, and anything else she might wish to do there. Letty jumped at the idea, and rushed away to change her clothes. Shortly after, brother and sister left Lyng House for Norwich in his lordship's phaeton, his lordship himself driving with his valet, Letty's maid, and the baggage following behind in a light travelling chaise.

For two days Sheldon and Letty forgot their past differences and their troubles, and enjoyed each other's company as they had never done before. Letty was amazed at her brother's vast knowledge of antiquities, and of his ability to fire enthusiasm in herself. She had never viewed the ancient city of Norwich with such interest. She was also amazed at what good company he could be, when he was not in an ill temper. He in turn was surprised how bright and intelligent Letty was, and what a happy, cheerful companion she was, for all her youth and sprightly disposition.

The brief respite was over too soon, at least for Sheldon and he returned to Lyng House with the problem of Josephine looming larger than ever. He supposed that by now Montagu would be well away in London, and it was high time he called at Roselands to talk to Josephine about what was to be done. He dreaded the prospect, but having made up his mind knew there was no turning back.

Accordingly, he rode over there first thing the next morning. He went with a heavy heart and black thoughts, cursing all women for the duplicity of two. The peace and beauty of the old Elizabethan manor house set in its tranquil moat amidst prim yew hedges did not accord with the turmoil he expected to find within. How often in the past three years had he come here with one thought only in mind, now it was the last thing he wanted. God, what a fool he had been!

He should have guessed how it was between Josephine and old Montagu. But, as he was the first to admit, he was not very perceptive where people were concerned.

Inside the house, the greatest shocks awaited him. The first was that no hysterical Josephine came rushing to meet him. The second was that he was shown into the library to be received by *Mr* Montagu, when he had expressly asked for *Mrs* Montagu. The old fellow had not gone to town, then, for here he was large as life, if a little pale, sitting up in his winged armchair by the fire, looking like a cat that had just had the cream.

"Ah, Langton, my dear young man, come in," Montagu greeted him warmly. "I have been expecting you these two or three days past."

"I have been away in Norwich with my sister," Sheldon said, feeling as if he had suddenly been plunged into a dream, or a nightmare. "I had not expected to find you at home, Montagu. I had thought you to be in town by now."

"And so I should had not a falling tree frightened my horse so that I was thrown

317

and knocked unconscious. They did not find me for some time. However, I have sustained nothing worse than a bump on the head and a slight chill."

"I am sorry to hear it, sir," Sheldon murmured politely, wondering what was coming next.

"A most fortunate accident, as it turns out, Langton, else I had gone away and never known till too late that Mrs Montagu — ahem — miscarried of her child the very same day I should have gone to town. My dear young man, a brandy for you, pray? You look as if you could do with it."

"So I could. Thank you," Sheldon said, feeling as if he had been knocked sideways. After the sheer hell he had been through on Josephine's account, for this to happen, of all things! How ironic was fate!

Mr Montagu poured brandy from the decanter on the occasional table at his elbow, and handed it to Sheldon urging him to be seated.

"And — how is Mrs Montagu?" the Marquis asked, gratefully tossing off the spirit.

"She will be right as ninepence in due course, I am happy to say. But she is not yet risen from her bed. She is naturally rather overset."

"Naturally," Sheldon agreed. A great relief was all he could confess to feeling, relief that he had had such a narrow escape. It would teach him to be much more careful in future.

"She does not wish to see you, sir," Montagu went on. "The accident to myself gave her such a fright, and with the loss of her child — the long and the short of it is, Langton, that she has come to her senses at last. She realizes how foolish was her infatuation for yourself, for a man who cared not a rap for her, and how she only wishes now to return to the love and security of her husband and children. You will have to look elsewhere for your pleasures in future, young man. But all's well that ends well, as the great Bard put it so aptly. I bear you no ill will, and trust we may be good neighbours in future. You see, I did not really want to lose my wife. Her miscarriage brought me to *my* senses. I might so easily have lost her altogether."

"I am very happy for you and Mrs Montagu, sir," Sheldon said formally, rising to his feet again. "Rest assured I shall not intrude upon either of you again except as a neighbour. Now, if you will forgive me, I have another call to make. Good-day to you, Montagu. Pray give my respects to your wife."

"I will. Good-day to *you*, Langton."

As Sheldon rode away from Roselands, he felt as if a great load had been lifted from his shoulders. Eagerly, he turned his horse's head towards Long Croft.

11

EVER since she had last seen Lord Langton, on that evening that had started so pleasantly and ended so terribly with the blowing up of the Lyng House pump-house, Rosalind Fenner-Smith has found herself thinking constantly of the Marquis, wondering how he went on, and wishing that she dared go and wait upon him again. But no excuse presented itself for calling at Lyng House, and she was so busy about other people's business that she had not the opportunity, in any event. Also, she did not trust herself where his lordship was concerned, for he disturbed her too greatly for her own peace of mind. She had seen the spark of desire in his own eyes, and she dreaded to think where it might all end. She had never counted on falling in love with any man, especially such a one as Lord Langton. She was only too aware of his faults, but equally so of his finer points. Yet, even though at present such a thing seemed highly unlikely, if he were ever to offer for her, she could not see herself as a member of Society, gracing balls and parties and heaven knows what, wasting away her days in idle luxury. She did not care for that idea at all. She wanted to be free to carry on her good works, to go on as she'd always done. Perhaps that's what came of being an old maid too long. And yet —

The day after the flood, news of Lord Langton's part in saving four of the villagers from drowning, of his generosity to all those who had suffered as a result of the floods, of his offer to help anyone hard hit by shortage of cash, and of his plan to renovate the church, not to mention his re-opening his park and, even more surprising, his scheme to give the village a model water supply, was the talk of the neighbourhood. It appeared that everyone had misjudged him, even over his action in the Rectory meadow that memorable night. He had merely been carrying out a survey to make sure his schemes harmed no one, indeed would prove beneficial to the community.

And just when he might have received a hero's ovation from his neighbours, he went off to Norwich with his sister. The matter of the trampled gardens and the damaged pump-house were conveniently forgotten, though there were not a few red faces in the area. The perpetrators of such misguided revenge breathed a sigh of relief, glad that the Marquis now seemed content to let sleeping dogs lie.

Mrs Fenner-Smith was as surprised as anyone when she heard the news.

"Well I never did, fancy that!" she commented. "That young man has turned out to be not such a bad penny, after all."

"I always knew he could not be such an evil monster as everyone made out," Rosalind asserted, inwardly glowing with happiness at the news, as much for Lord Langton's sake as for confirmation of her belief in him. "Which just proves one should not listen to gossip. The thing about Lord Langton, Mamma, is that he has to be handled right. It is so easy to set his back up, and then he flies off the handle, and is deliberately contrary."

"To be sure, you seem to understand him exceeding well, my dear," Mrs Fenner-Smith remarked, giving her daughter an odd look, but Rosalind turned away, and would not be drawn out on the subject.

And then a letter arrived for Captain Fenner-Smith, which threw the family at Long Croft into turmoil.

"Good gracious, Uncle, whatever is amiss?" Rosalind cried, seeing her uncle's stricken look. "Are you unwell again, pray?"

"No, no, my dear, it is nothing," the Captain hastened to assure her. "The shock merely, though I have known of it for a while. But now the moment is almost upon us — "

"What, are we about to be invaded by the French at last!" his sister-in-law exclaimed in dismay. "Oh, do not say so!"

"Nothing so dramatic or terrible as that, I assure you," the Captain said, smiling faintly. "It is my — my wife. She is due to arrive here tomorrow."

"Oh!"

Mother and daughter looked at each

other, not quite knowing what to say. Had they outstayed their welcome at Long Croft? Would it be best if they went? Or did the Captain need their support at such a time?

"Pray, do not think this means you have to go," Michael said quickly, noting their uneasiness. "This is your home for as long as you wish. Besides, I know not what her purpose is in coming back to me, whether she means to stay — "

"Or whether indeed you *want* her back, surely, Uncle," Rosalind insisted firmly. "It was she left you, recollect, and she has been away so long, you can be under no obligation to have her back if you do not wish to."

"Precisely, my dear. But I was ever a weak man, and she *is* my wife still, at least in law. But that is not the whole of it. My God, I wish I knew what to do — "

His sister-in-law and niece exchanged glances, this time of perplexity, while the Captain limped away and shut himself in his study.

"Ever since he first heard from your aunt, something seems to have been bothering him greatly," Mrs Fenner-Smith remarked. "Something beyond the actual fact of the possibility of her return. Oh dear, I wonder what it can be? I do wish he would confide in us. But he was ever a close man, even with your poor dear Papa."

The rest of the day was spent in making rather frantic preparations for the other Mrs Fenner-Smith's arrival. Even Polly, despite her condition and recent indisposition, set to with a will, determined to prove her worth to these good people who had so kindly taken her in and cared for her. Wherever Miss Rosalind went in future, she decided, she would go too, if she'd have her. And she'd never go to bed with a man again unless he seemed like to marry her. She'd learnt *her* lesson.

The next morning, as the Long Croft family, on tenterhooks, awaited the arrival of their long-lost relative, Lord Langton descended upon them. He was the last person they expected to see, believing him to be still away in Norwich.

For Sheldon, it was to prove a rather disastrous visit. For a start, Polly opened the door to him. He had forgotten she now worked there, and to be suddenly confronted by her, her belly swelling with his child, was enough to put him off his stroke. At such a time, the last thing he wanted to be reminded of was Polly. Why the devil did Miss Smith have to place her here, right under his nose, where he was a constant visitor? Why, if she had to practise her charity on his ex-doxy, could she not have sent the hussy away somewhere? Could she not have had more sensibility, or had she done it deliberately to try and punish him for his using of Polly?

Polly was as pertly pretty as ever, but he no longer desired her. To cover his displeasure and slight embarrassment at seeing her, he addressed her with cold aloofness, and was agreeably surprised when she replied with all proper respect, just as if they had never enjoyed those pleasurable skirmishes between the sheets together. No doubt Miss Smith had given the chit a thorough dressing-down and put her in her place.

The next blow to Lord Langton was when he discovered that he had walked in at rather an inopportune moment at Long Croft, the family being all prepared for a very different visitor. The Captain, in particular, seemed to be in a very nervous state, and only too anxious for him to be gone, though he did not say as much.

"I beg your pardon," Sheldon apologized, a little put out. "I had not meant to intrude upon you at such a time. Only I have not seen any of you for such an age, and I thought merely to see how you all did. I shall not stop."

"No, pray do not go quite so soon," Rosalind begged, at once sensing his huffiness. "We are not so ragmannered, do not think it. We are prodigious pleased to see you, to be sure." Coming up close to him, she added in an undertone: "You must forgive my poor uncle his seeming rudeness. He is a trifle overwrought. Come into the back parlour, and drink a glass of madeira with me."

"Thank you," he said gratefully following her down the dark hall. "In any event, it was really *you* I wanted to see. You have kept away from me for so long. Have I done anything to offend you?"

Beneath her lumpy figure and shapeless black dress her heart was beginning to bump uncomfortably. Her limbs felt shaky, and she was breaking out in a cold sweat. Surely he was not going to declare himself now, of all times? And it was so soon. They had not known each other above a month.

"No, of course you have done nothing to offend me, sir," she replied, trying to sound cheerful. "How can you think so? I am not easily offended, you know." Even his voice gave her a thrill, so well-modulated and cultured as it was, unlike her own harsh tones with their slight London accent. How could such a man, so well-looking, so fashionably elegant, so clever and cultured, possibly care for a female like her? She must surely have imagined it. It was all wishful thinking. His next words belied that notion.

"I have missed you devilishly, Miss Smith," he said, very gently. "But there were reasons why I could not wait upon you before. Now those reasons are gone, and I am free to speak my mind to you. Though I must confess I scarce know what to say. I scarce know myself what

I feel about you. I made a fool of myself once before by loving a woman. I do not want to make the same mistake twice. That is why I am so unsure of myself. But I *do* know, my dear Miss Smith, that were you to go away right now I should be desolate indeed. You make me happy, which no other woman has ever been able to do, not since — since my fiancée jilted me all those years ago. Not only that, for that does indeed sound a selfish reason for liking you. I admire you for your spirit, for your good works, your kindness and tolerance, particularly of my own shortcomings, your ability to cope with everything and everyone and every situation. I even dare to hope — think — that in some measure you return my regard. If I did not, I should not dare approach you, for I am persuaded you would slap me down at once. At this stage I cannot honourably offer for you, for I am too uncertain of myself, and my heart is still too sore. But I should like to know if you could ever look kindly on my suit, if I might hope that one day — "
He broke off, ending in a low voice: "I promise one thing, my dear, I'd always

be faithful to you."

During all this time, neither of them had heard the scrunch of carriage wheels coming up the back drive. Indeed, for a moment, time had seemed to stand still for them both. Rosalind had stood quite still while he spoke, her back turned to him, her hand on the decanter of madeira. Now she faced him, her eyes glowing, her beautiful skin a delicate shade of pink. She placed her large, rather rough hand on his arm, and was about to tell him what was in her heart, when the door was thrust open, and a small, dark, very fashionably dressed young woman walked into the room. Rosalind fell back in embarrassed dismay. The newcomer stopped short, an expression of supercilious triumph on her hard, lovely features. Sheldon remained rooted to the spot in shock and incredulity, all the colour gone from his face, the look in his dark eyes betraying the pain and anguish of his soul.

"My God!" he gasped faintly. "Amelia! What in heaven's name are you doing here?"

"Did I catch you in a compromising

situation?" the stranger said, in a hard, mocking voice. "My poor Sheldon, to be caught out so by me, of all people. Did you not know? I wrote my husband that I would arrive today?"

"Your — your *husband*?" Sheldon cried, unable to believe his ears.

"That's what I said. My husband, Captain Fenner Smith. How odd that after so long my husband should come to live on your doorstep. I quite thought he had told you by now. How remiss of him! What a surprise for you to run across me in such an outlandish spot. Dear Sheldon, pray don't look so dazed. I have not come back for you. You are the last man on earth I want, thank you."

Seeing that Lord Langton was about to either break down or explode with anger, Rosalind, though she did not quite as yet comprehend what was between these two, stepped forward quickly.

"You must be Aunt Amelia," she said, her voice at its most strident. "Of course you are expected. We were in receipt of your letter yesterday."

Amelia glanced up and down Rosalind

with undisguised disdain.

"I must say, Sheldon," she remarked, "your taste in women has vastly deteriorated. And as for you, ma'am, I do not care to be called 'Aunt' by a woman who looks to be quite as old as myself."

"How dare you, Amelia — " Sheldon began furiously, beginning to recover himself somewhat.

"Oh, I beg your pardon! I had quite forgot you seem to be enamoured of the creature, gazing into her eyes like a love-sick swain."

"I think, ma'am," Sheldon said icily, with marvellous self-restraint, "that you should know that this young lady is your husband's niece, the only child of his brother, and therefore his heir."

"Heaven forbid!" Amelia exclaimed with mock faintness.

Suddenly Sheldon felt a great release from the hurt and bondage that this woman had imposed on him all these years. In a flash his eyes were opened, and he saw her for what she was, a vain, empty, capricious, self-seeking, self-centred bitch, who had no more cared for him than she had doubtless cared for Captain Fenner-Smith. She no longer had the power to hurt him, and his youthful love for her was killed stone dead. Rosalind, his fair Rosalind, lumpy and shapeless and horse-faced as she might be, was all he wanted. He could almost laugh out loud at the irony of it all.

"It is what I have been wanting to tell you ever since I first knew she was coming back, Langton," the Captain's voice came from the doorway. "But I could not summon up the courage. It was cowardly of me, I know. Only I like you too well to want to lose either your friendship or your good opinion of me."

"All along you knew that your wife and my ex-fiancée were one and the same?" Sheldon cried, still rather bemused.

"I fear so. I first sought your company, that day I met you, by my front gate, because I felt I owed you something, was responsible for the hurt you received at Amelia's hands."

"Owed me something?" Sheldon did laugh out loud this time, much to everyone's amazement. "My God, sir, it is *I* owe *you* something, for saving me from a lifetime of regret and misery. Can you conceive of being hitched to that abomination of a woman for life?"

"That, alas, my friend, is my fate, for my folly," the Captain said sadly.

"Pray do not be put about on my account," Amelia put in haughtily. "If you think I could bear to live so near such a sad heartless wretch as my Lord Langton, or eke out my days in this — this monstrous cottage with a wreck of a man like the Captain, you are out of your minds. I have come to make sure my poor ailing husband is well as can be expected, and to make sure," she added viciously, "that now he is to be *Sir* Michael Fenner-Smith one of these fine days, he does not try to do me out of my rightful title and inheritance as his wife."

"Rest assured, I shall not do that, Amelia," the Captain said, propelling her from the room. "You shall have anything you want, if only you will go away again and leave me to my solitude."

"Well, one thing," his wife retorted spitefully, "you will get no further heirs out of that whey-faced niece of yours. With a face like that, she will never catch a husband."

"There you are far out, Amelia," Sheldon spoke up firmly. "Miss Fenner-Smith has already *caught*, as you so crudely put it, a husband. Myself. If she will have me, that is." He turned to look anxiously at Rosalind, who had come to his side again, and once more had her hand on his arm.

"My dear friend, is this true?" the Captain said in incredulous delight. "Niece, what say you? Will you have his lordship?"

"Of course, Uncle," Rosalind said bluntly, "else who will make sure he does not fall out with his neighbours again, or leave the serving maids alone, or — "

"Or *love* him?" Sheldon added, as Crazy Mick pushed his wife out the door and followed after her. "*Do* you love me, Rosalind?"

"Well, of course," she answered promptly and practically, "or why should I bother with you?"

"I thought perhaps because you consider

me one of your worthy causes?" he retorted, half teasing, half serious.

"Well, that too, I own. You will take much putting up with at times. You really must try and curb that dreadful temper of yours."

"I'll try, I promise, my love. God, how I could ever have lost so much as one night's sleep, let alone a dozen years of nights, over that other creature, I cannot conceive. I must have been mad or blind or both."

"Poor Papa really stirred up a hornet's nest by getting killed, did he not?" Rosalind laughed. She was serious again at once. "Only when we are married, you will not stop me from doing my good works, will you, Sheldon?" she asked anxiously.

He closed his arms about her, and held her tight.

"Of course not, my love. You without your good works? Why, I do declare you may even get me to assist you at times. Rosalind, my fair Rosalind. How I love you."

And he kissed her.

Other titles in the
Ulverscroft Large Print Series:

TO FIGHT THE WILD
Rod Ansell and Rachel Percy

Lost in uncharted Australian bush, Rod Ansell survived by hunting and trapping wild animals, improvising shelter and using all the bushman's skills he knew.

COROMANDEL
Pat Barr

India in the 1830s is a hot, uncomfortable place, where the East India Company still rules. Amelia and her new husband find themselves caught up in the animosities which seethe between the old order and the new.

THE SMALL PARTY
Lillian Beckwith

A frightening journey to safety begins for Ruth and her small party as their island is caught up in the dangers of armed insurrection.

THE WILDERNESS WALK
Sheila Bishop

Stifling unpleasant memories of a misbegotten romance in Cleave with Lord Francis Aubrey, Lavinia goes on holiday there with her sister. The two women are thrust into a romantic intrigue involving none other than Lord Francis.

THE RELUCTANT GUEST
Rosalind Brett

Ann Calvert went to spend a month on a South African farm with Theo Borland and his sister. They both proved to be different from her first idea of them, and there was Storr Peterson — the most disturbing man she had ever met.

ONE ENCHANTED SUMMER
Anne Tedlock Brooks

A tale of mystery and romance and a girl who found both during one enchanted summer.

CLOUD OVER MALVERTON
Nancy Buckingham

Dulcie soon realises that something is seriously wrong at Malverton, and when violence strikes she is horrified to find herself under suspicion of murder.

AFTER THOUGHTS
Max Bygraves

The Cockney entertainer tells stories of his East End childhood, of his RAF days, and his post-war showbusiness successes and friendships with fellow comedians.

MOONLIGHT
AND MARCH ROSES
D. Y. Cameron

Lynn's search to trace a missing girl takes her to Spain, where she meets Clive Hendon. While untangling the situation, she untangles her emotions and decides on her own future.

NURSE ALICE IN LOVE
Theresa Charles

Accepting the post of nurse to little Fernie Sherrod, Alice Everton could not guess at the romance, suspense and danger which lay ahead at the Sherrod's isolated estate.

POIROT INVESTIGATES
Agatha Christie

Two things bind these eleven stories together — the brilliance and uncanny skill of the diminutive Belgian detective, and the stupidity of his Watson-like partner, Captain Hastings.

LET LOOSE THE TIGERS
Josephine Cox

Queenie promised to find the long-lost son of the frail, elderly murderess, Hannah Jason. But her enquiries threatened to unlock the cage where crucial secrets had long been held captive.

THE TWILIGHT MAN
Frank Gruber

Jim Rand lives alone in the California desert awaiting death. Into his hermit existence comes a teenage girl who blows both his past and his brief future wide open.

DOG IN THE DARK
Gerald Hammond

Jim Cunningham breeds and trains gun dogs, and his antagonism towards the devotees of show spaniels earns him many enemies. So when one of them is found murdered, the police are on his doorstep within hours.

THE RED KNIGHT
Geoffrey Moxon

When he finds himself a pawn on the chessboard of international espionage with his family in constant danger, Guy Trent becomes embroiled in moves and countermoves which may mean life or death for Western scientists.

TIGER TIGER
Frank Ryan

A young man involved in drugs is found murdered. This is the first event which will draw Detective Inspector Sandy Woodings into a whirlpool of murder and deceit.

CAROLINE MINUSCULE
Andrew Taylor

Caroline Minuscule, a medieval script, is the first clue to the whereabouts of a cache of diamonds. The search becomes a deadly kind of fairy story in which several murders have an other-worldly quality.

LONG CHAIN OF DEATH
Sarah Wolf

During the Second World War four American teenagers from the same town join the Army together. Forty-two years later, the son of one of the soldiers realises that someone is systematically wiping out the families of the four men.

THE LISTERDALE MYSTERY
Agatha Christie

Twelve short stories ranging from the light-hearted to the macabre, diverse mysteries ingeniously and plausibly contrived and convincingly unravelled.

TO BE LOVED
Lynne Collins

Andrew married the woman he had always loved despite the knowledge that Sarah married him for reasons of her own. So much heartache could have been avoided if only he had known how vital it was to be loved.

ACCUSED NURSE
Jane Converse

Paula found herself accused of a crime which could cost her her job, her nurse's reputation, and even the man she loved, unless the truth came to light.

BUTTERFLY MONTANE
Dorothy Cork

Parma had come to New Guinea to marry Alec Rivers, but she found him completely disinterested and that overbearing Pierce Adams getting entirely the wrong idea about her.

HONOURABLE FRIENDS
Janet Daley

Priscilla Burford is happily married when she meets Junior Environment Minister Alistair Thurston. Inevitably, sexual obsession and political necessity collide.

WANDERING MINSTRELS
Mary Delorme

Stella Wade's career as a concert pianist might have been ruined by the rudeness of a famous conductor, so it seemed to her agent and benefactor. Even Sir Nicholas fails to see the possibilities when John Tallis falls deeply in love with Stella.

MORNING IS BREAKING
Lesley Denny

The growing frenzy of war catapults Diane Clements into a clandestine marriage and separation with a German refugee.

LAST BUS TO WOODSTOCK
Colin Dexter

A girl's body is discovered huddled in the courtyard of a Woodstock pub, and Detective Chief Inspector Morse and Sergeant Lewis are hunting a rapist and a murderer.

THE STUBBORN TIDE
Anne Durham

Everyone advised Carol not to grieve so excessively over her cousin's death. She might have followed their advice if the man she loved thought that way about her, but another girl came first in his affections.